'I couldn't help them, James,' said Lisa, looking up, staring at him, wide-eyed, like a frightened animal. 'I've tried. I've tried to remember but I can't. They keep asking questions about the colour of the car. The registration number. The driver. But I don't remember. I don't remember anything at all. I don't even remember being there. I only know what I was told. That they found me in the ditch. I don't know how I got there. They reckon I must have jumped as the car came towards us. I must have jumped out of the way, James. I must have done! And it didn't hit me. It hit her. And now she's . . .'

'Please,' said James. 'Please don't make it worse. Don't blame yourself, Lisa.'

'I don't have to,' said Lisa. 'Kits knows. She knows what happened. She blames me. That's why she won't see me . . .'

www.booksattransworld.co.uk/childrens

Also available by Sandra Glover, and published by Corgi Books:

BREAKING THE RULES
THE NOWHERE BOY

THE GIRL WHO KNEW

Sandra Glover

CORGI BOOKS

THE GIRL WHO KNEW
A CORGI BOOK : 0 552 546992

First published in Great Britain by Andersen Press Limited

PRINTING HISTORY
Andersen Press edition published 2000
Corgi edition published 2001

3 5 7 9 10 8 6 4 2

Set in 12/14½pt Bembo by
Phoenix Typesetting, Ilkley, West Yorkshire.

Corgi Books are published by Transworld Publishers,
61–63 Uxbridge Road, London W5 5SA,
a division of The Random House Group Ltd,
in Australia by Random House Australia (Pty) Ltd,
20 Alfred Street, Milsons Point, Sydney, NSW 2061, Australia,
in New Zealand by Random House New Zealand Ltd,
18 Poland Road, Glenfield, Auckland 10, New Zealand
and in South Africa by Random House (Pty) Ltd,
Endulini, 5a Jubilee Road, Parktown 2193, South Africa

Made and printed in Great Britain by
Cox & Wyman Ltd, Reading, Berkshire.

CHAPTER ONE

The pain was fading now. Almost gone. Only the memory of it remained. Kits tried sitting up and was surprised by how easy it was. It was amazing. She felt better. Totally better.

She swung her feet over the side of the hard bed and tried to put them on the floor. She found only empty space. The bed was impossibly high off the ground. She tried supporting herself on her hands so she could drop down. Kits was so absorbed by this activity that, for a moment, she registered nothing about her surroundings or the other people in the room.

The whiteness was what she noticed first. The bright, clean whiteness of the room. The shining chrome and white surfaces of the machines. Lots of machines. Then the smell. The antiseptic smell which reminded her of the stuff her mum put down the loo or the ointment you put on bee stings. Possibly both, mingled in a strange perfume, dominating the room.

Finally, she noticed the people. Or rather the

eyes. Half a dozen pairs of eyes, staring intently above the masks. Eyes belonging to people with gloved hands and weird robes.

She should have been frightened. But she wasn't. She knew she was in hospital. And hospitals weren't scary. She'd been brought up with hospitals. Grandma Joyce used to be a nurse, before she retired. Maybe this was her old hospital. Maybe not. It didn't matter. Hospitals were fine. Especially when they made you better. And she was certainly better.

She pushed with her hands and slipped down until she felt the cold floor against her bare feet. She walked, slowly, round the room, expecting the eyes to follow her. Expecting gasps of admiration at her progress. She barely noticed when it didn't happen. It was enough to be up, walking, pushing open the door, strolling out on to a corridor filled with bright light. Brighter than she'd ever seen.

Walking slowly, she tried to follow the source of the light, burning hypnotically in the distance, drawing her towards it. But the more she walked the further away it seemed to get. She tried walking more quickly, determined to reach it. It made no difference. It was out of her grasp and she was rapidly becoming exhausted.

Trying to do too much too soon. What was it her dad always said about her?

'You always want to run, before you can walk, Kits.'

Maybe it was true. She'd always been hyper-active. Always in a hurry. Wanting to do everything. Try everything. Not like her brothers. Calm, relaxed, easy-going, the pair of them.

Well, she'd over-stretched herself, this time. She couldn't go on. It was too far. Too long a journey. Couldn't go back either. Her legs had simply stopped working.

It occurred to her that it would be nicer to float. Glide back down the corridor and slip into bed. The thought was enough. Her body rose effortlessly into the air, sailed back down the corridor, through the door and hovered above the bed.

Wrong bed. This bed was already occupied. Wrong room, surely? There was an operation in progress. You couldn't just stroll – or float – into an operating theatre, could you? She wanted to leave but her eyes refused to search for the door. They looked, instead, at the patient. A young person. Someone whose features she couldn't see clearly but who was terrifyingly familiar. In the instant that she recognized herself, there on the operating table, her other self dropped like a stone.

A dream. It was a dream, of course. She knew that as soon as she felt the jolt of her dream body, merging with the real one. She had tried to open her eyes, there and then, but her real body wouldn't let her.

They were open now, though. How long had it

7

been? And where was she? Not in the operating theatre. In a bed. A proper bed. The room was hazy and seemed to sway as if adrift in a sea mist. After-effects of the anaesthetic she must have had, obviously. Still, it wasn't pleasant. Not like in the dream she so desperately wanted to return to.

She was about to cry out, when she felt the pressure of a hand clutching her own. She blinked rapidly, then forced her eyes wide open, peering through the mist, trying to make sense of the shape beside her which wouldn't quite come into focus. Chair shape. Person shape. Grey hair. Smiling eyes. Hazel, like her own.

'Grandad?'

'Hello, Kits.'

Kits. Grandad had called her Kitten from the minute he saw her as a tiny baby. Gradually, as she got older, it had been shortened to Kits. The whole family used it now. So did her friends. She only ever got Katherine from teachers or new acquaintances.

'Where am I?'

It sounded stupid, like some dated medical drama.

'I think you know where you are.'

Not the answer she expected. Not really the person she expected. She tried again.

'Where's Mum?'

'Not far. You'll see her soon.'

'What happened?'

She'd definitely seen too many medical programmes. She was asking all the silly questions. Not that Grandad seemed to mind.

'The accident, Kits. The car accident. Do you remember?'

She nodded. Then shook her head, not wanting to remember.

'It's all right, love. You're going to be all right, now. You know that, don't you?'

She nodded again.

'I feel so tired, though. And it hurts. The pain's come back.'

'It will pass, Kits. You'll soon be better. I promise.'

She was already beginning to feel better. Just looking at him. Holding his hand. But it wasn't like the dream. She'd felt wonderful then. So healthy. So alive. She closed her eyes, willing the dream to come back. So she could float, escape the pain.

'No, Kits,' Grandad said firmly. 'You mustn't go back to sleep now. It's time to wake up. Your mum's waiting to see you. They're all waiting. You want to see them, don't you?'

'Yes,' said Kits. 'Yes, I do.'

She felt his hand release her own.

'Don't go. You don't need to go,' she cried out, suddenly afraid.

'Yes. I must, Kitten,' he said. 'The others want to see you. Now you're ready. I was only looking after you, while you slept.'

Kits smiled. It was like in the old days, when she was a little girl. Her grandparents would come to babysit when her mum and dad went out. Her brother, James, would sleep right through the night. Lewis too, even when he was a baby. But she would always wake up from some nightmare. Cry out. In an instant, Grandad would be there.

'It's all right,' he would say. 'It was only a dream. I'm looking after you. Nothing can harm you. Go back to sleep.'

She supposed he must have said something like that before he left because she seemed to have drifted back to sleep. By the time she woke again they'd moved her to a different room. Much more normal. Pink, flowery curtains. Green cover on the bed. Washbasin in the corner. Or maybe it was the same room and she was seeing it more clearly, now that the mist had disappeared. Or the drugs had worn off.

Strangely she saw the wider picture before she took in the group clustered round her bed. Mum. Dad. James. Lewis. Just as Grandad had promised. They weren't as calm as he had been. They were all standing, as if they'd recently been pacing the room and had turned to stone, the minute her eyes opened. Anxiety screamed out from their faces, though it affected them in different ways. James's screwed-up forehead made him look older than seventeen. Lewis, with his fist stuck in his mouth, seemed much younger than his ten years. Mum's white face looked thinner than ever. Dad's eyes had sunk into deep, black hollows.

And what about her? If they looked that bad, how on earth did she look to them?

'Kits?' said her mother, tentatively stretching out her hand to touch Kits' arm. 'Are you . . . can you . . . how . . . ?'

'Hi, Mum.'

The words came out weaker, fainter, than she'd meant but they had a devastating effect. Lewis burst into tears. James grabbed hold of Mum's shoulders as she started to sway and eased her into a chair, before dropping onto his knees beside the bed, as if in prayer. Dad rushed over, sat on the other side of the bed and grabbed Kits' hand, squeezing tighter than Grandad had done.

'Hey,' she said, smiling.

'Sorry. I'm just so . . . I mean it's been . . . How are you, Kits? How do you *feel*?'

'I don't know. I don't feel anything much.'

Awkward, embarrassed glances passed around the bed.

'No pain?'

'A bit. Not so bad.'

'You've had a lot of drugs. To keep it down. Until things start to heal.'

'What sort of things, Dad? What's happened? It's been so strange, I can't seem to remember . . .'

'The doctors said there might be some memory loss. We were terrified you wouldn't even know us.'

'I wasn't,' said Lewis, drying his tears with his sleeve. 'I knew you wouldn't forget my ugly mug. Whatever happened.'

Kits smiled. She was always getting at Lewis. Always winding him up. But they were close. Closer even than she was to James, though she was only two years younger than James and they had spent five years together before Lewis made an unexpected addition to the family.

'So,' said her dad, cautiously. 'Can you remember . . . other things . . . ordinary things? Where you live?'

The image came to Kits' mind immediately. Three-storey house on the edge of town. Long garden. High wall hiding the canal that ran behind it. Ginger sitting on the fence, on the lookout for birds and mice in the hedges by the towpath. No problems there.

'Yes,' she said. 'I remember everything . . . I think. Home. My room. School. The cat. My birthday, the . . . I'm sorry . . . it's hard to talk. I'm tired and it hurts when I move my mouth.'

'You're doing great, Kits,' said her dad. 'But don't over-stretch yourself. The doctors say you'll need plenty of rest.'

'I know,' said Kits. 'Don't try to run before I can walk.'

More embarrassed, anxious glances.

'You'll be fine, love,' said her mother. 'Whatever happens. We're here to look after you. You're through the worst. You'll be all right now.'

'I know,' said Kits, trying to talk without moving her lips too much, so it didn't hurt. 'That's what Grandad said.'

'Grandad?'

'When I woke up, before. He must have told you.'

Her mother said 'Grandad and Grandma Helen were on holiday. In America, when it happened. Visiting those friends, remember? Of course, they booked a flight back as soon as they heard and then they'll drive up from London. But it's too soon . . . they couldn't have got here . . . not without us knowing.'

Kits understood the mistake, immediately. She didn't mean Grandma Helen and Grandad Bill. Her mother's parents. She'd never been so close to them. Never had a chance. They were hardly ever in the country. Life was one long foreign holiday to them.

Nice of them to be flying home, though. Not that they needed to. She didn't feel too bad. Just tired. Very, very . . .

She realized she was drifting off again and pulled herself round.

'Not Grandad Bill,' she explained. 'Grandad David.'

In the silence which followed, she wondered what she'd said wrong. Then suddenly, it was all being explained with awful clarity. What she should have know all along. If she'd bothered to search her memory properly.

'Not Grandad David,' her mother was saying. 'You couldn't have seen David. He . . . last year . . . his heart . . .'

'I know, Mum,' said Kits, starting to cry. 'I know now. I remember. He died, didn't he? Grandad David is dead. But it doesn't make any difference. I saw him. He was looking after me.'

CHAPTER TWO

Kits tried to push herself up on her pillows but pain ripped through her shoulders, forcing her to slump back, frustrated and angry.

It had been four days since the operation. Four agonizing days of lying still, wired up to goodness knows how many contraptions and swallowing painkillers every couple of hours. When would she be out of here? When would she be allowed out of bed?

'Mum,' she screamed out. 'Mum!'

Where had everyone got to? One minute, it seemed, she'd had a roomful of people and the next they'd all disappeared. Just when she needed them.

She raised her hand to her face and touched it gently. The effort of shouting for Mum had set off a throbbing around her jawbone. Her face was still bruised, slightly swollen and she could trace the lines of the cuts with her fingertips, zigzagging across her cheeks, along her nose and around her mouth. Goodness knows what she must look like, she thought, bitterly. They wouldn't let her near a mirror. Not yet.

'You're lucky,' one of the nurses had told her cheerfully only a couple of hours ago. 'The injuries to your face are only superficial. They'll heal in time. You won't need plastic surgery. You won't have any permanent scars.'

Maybe not scars, no. But what about the other stuff? The stuff they weren't telling her? What about her legs? Why couldn't she feel them? Why couldn't she move? Why couldn't she even drag herself six centimetres higher on the pillows?

'Mum! Mum! Mum!'

It wasn't her mother, but James, who finally appeared in response to her call.

'Where've you been? Where's Mum?'

'You fell asleep,' said James. 'Just after five when me and Lewis turned up so we've been having a sandwich in the snack bar and Mum's been called in to see the doctor.'

'Well, I'm awake now and I want to sit up,' said Kits, pushing down with her hands again.

'Keep still,' said James. 'I'll lift you.'

'I don't want to be lifted,' she snapped, as James helped to raise her into a more comfortable position. 'I want to be able to do it myself. I want to be able to move. What's wrong with me, James? Why can't I move? Why won't anybody tell me?

The doctor must have said something, by now.'

'He hasn't said anything,' James lied. 'They don't know. Not for definite. Anyway, I've got some news. I've just bumped into someone out there. You've got a visitor.'

'Lisa. It's Lisa, isn't it?'

'Yes,' said James, surprised that Kits had guessed so easily. 'Feel up to seeing her yet?'

'No,' Kits snapped. 'Look at me! Do you think I want people coming in here gawping?'

'You don't look too bad. Not now. Swelling's gone down a lot round the eyes. And besides Lisa's not coming to gawp. She's been dying to see you. I know you're not to have too many visitors yet, but Lisa's your best friend . . .'

'She was,' said Kits, pointedly.

James frowned, trying to understand Kits' changed attitude to her friend, which had slowly been revealing itself over the past couple of days.

'Kits, this isn't like you,' James protested. 'Surely you don't blame Lisa? It wasn't her fault . . .'

'Wasn't it? So how come she's fine, James? How come she escaped with barely a scratch? How come the car hit me full on and never touched her, James? Just tell me that.'

'I don't know,' said James. 'Nobody does. Lisa doesn't remember anything . . .'

'How convenient.'

'And you haven't been up to talking about it,' said James, trying to ignore the venom in his sister's voice.

'Just because I haven't talked about it doesn't mean I don't think about it,' she hissed. 'I see those headlights every minute of every flaming day. I feel the impact over and over, jolting me out of sleep every time I try to close my eyes. And I see *her*, James. Leaping out of the way to save her own, miserable skin. So don't tell me what to think, who to blame.'

James squeezed his sister's hand.

'I'm sorry,' he said, feeling his words to be hopelessly inadequate. 'I'll tell Lisa . . . maybe later, when you feel . . .'

'Don't bother,' said Kits. 'Just tell her what I told you to tell her yesterday and the day before and the day before that. Just tell her, no. I don't want to see her. Not ever.'

Lisa was pacing up and down on the corridor when James came out. One look at his face was enough. She turned away, not wanting him to see the tears.

'Wait,' he said. 'Lisa, wait.'

She stopped, turned, tried to wipe her eyes on her jacket sleeve, but he had seen.

'Please,' he said. 'Please don't take it personally. Kits . . . I mean, she isn't herself at the moment . . . we couldn't expect . . .'

'Does she know yet?' Lisa blurted out. 'Does she know all of it?'

'Not really,' said James. 'Not yet. We haven't . . . She knows she can't move her legs, of course. Knows there's no feeling. But she thinks it's temporary. Keeps asking when she'll be able to get up.'

'Shouldn't someone . . . ?'

'It's not easy, Lisa,' said James, trying not to snap. 'Mum tried yesterday but she couldn't. I mean, you haven't known Kits that long but you know what she's like . . . how do you tell someone like Kits that she might never . . .'

He lapsed into silence. Lisa followed suit. There was no way to answer the unfinished question. James was right. She hadn't known Kits long. Less than a year, she thought, doing a quick calculation. It was February now. She and her family had moved to the area at the end of last July. So about seven months.

'Katherine will help you settle in,' Lisa's new teacher had said.

But Kits had done far more than that. She had talked Lisa into joining the netball team. Persuaded her to go to swimming lessons. Dragged her along to Youth Club with the promise of making lots of new friends.

It had all sounded dreadful to Lisa, at first. She'd always been shy. Even when she was small. Even when she was happy. Before all the trouble began.

Before her parents split up. And later, after what happened with Ross, she'd withdrawn even more, terrified of mixing with people. Scared of getting too close.

And as for outdoor pursuits! She'd protested to Kits that she was clumsy, one of life's natural couch potatoes. But Kits had only laughed, drawing Lisa in with infectious enthusiasm. Lisa had found herself doing things with Kits that she'd never dreamt of before. Abseiling, for heaven's sake! Caving!

That was when she'd first met James. James was into caving. So there she'd been in her scruffiest jeans, jacket padded out with several layers of jumpers, hair tied back in a ponytail, staring at the most gorgeous bloke she'd ever seen. All six foot two of him, topped with the blond hair and the sparkling hazel eyes which characterized the whole family.

Not that it mattered much what she wore. James barely noticed her, in or out of caves. To him, she was just his kid sister's mate. And of course, she'd always been too shy to really talk to him. Not that he was particularly intimidating, thought Lisa, looking at him now, staring down at her, his eyes full of concern.

He was always friendly. He always smiled at her. You couldn't help but like him. In fact it was impossible to dislike any of the Bellinghams. Even Lewis with his childish tricks. They'd become like a second family to her, Lisa thought. A nice, normal happy family like the ones that beamed out at you on adverts for breakfast cereal.

Their clean, pleasant house was a place to escape to when things got tough at home. A place where you could forget the past and pretend to be happy again. All because of Kits. And now?

Now it was over. No more pretending. No more happy families. The accident had changed everything . . . for all of them . . . for ever.

She felt James put his arm round her shoulder, as her whole body started to tremble.

'Can I get you anything?' he asked. 'The coffee from the machine's not bad.'

'No,' said Lisa. 'No thanks. I'll be OK. Honest. I ought to be going. Mum panics more than ever now, when I'm out late. I'll phone tomorrow . . .'

James nodded.

'I could phone you, if you want,' he said.

'No,' said Lisa, hastily, not wanting to explain why that wasn't possible. 'I'll phone the ward. Usually I get to talk to your mum. She keeps me informed.'

'OK.'

'There was one other thing,' said Lisa, as James turned towards Kits' room. 'Your mum said yesterday that Kits is still talking about the dream . . . the lights, the floating, seeing her grandad and stuff . . .'

'Yeah,' said James. 'It wouldn't be too bad if she accepted it was a dream. But she still insists it was real. The doctor said she'll forget about it in time, though,' he added hopefully. 'It'll fade eventually . . . dreams do . . . don't they?'

'So they reckon there's no brain damage,' said Lisa, anxiously.

'No,' said James. 'Not damage, as such. She's still twice as sharp as me and Lew put together, thank goodness. But the doctors say there could have been some neurological trauma that didn't show up on the scans. That's why we've got to be careful. She's not to get worked up . . . we've been told not to talk about the accident, unless she mentions it first.'

'But surely the police will want to interview her?' said Lisa.

'Soon,' said James. 'The doctors have been putting them off. I mean we all want that driver caught but, to be honest, Kits hasn't been up to it.'

'Neither have I,' said Lisa. 'But that doesn't stop them. They haven't left me alone! They were round again yesterday.'

'And?' James prompted, as Lisa fell silent, her head hanging down.

'I couldn't help them, James,' said Lisa, looking up, staring at him, wide-eyed, like a frightened animal. 'I've tried. I've tried to remember but I can't. They keep asking questions about the colour of the car. The registration number. The driver. But

I don't remember. I don't remember anything at all. I don't even remember being there. I only know what I was told. That they found me in the ditch. I don't know how I got there. They reckon I must have jumped as the car came towards us. I must have jumped out of the way, James. I must have done! And it didn't hit me. It hit her. And now she's . . .'

'Please,' said James. 'Please don't make it worse. Don't blame yourself, Lisa.'

'I don't have to,' said Lisa. 'Kits knows. She knows what happened. She blames me. That's why she won't see me.'

'Lisa,' said James firmly. 'Kits isn't herself. She'll come round in time. So what if you jumped? It was a reflex action. Anybody would. You wouldn't have time to think. It's a natural reaction. There's only one person to blame,' he added, bitterly. 'The driver of that car. The maniac who hit Kits and then drove off. And the best way you can help yourself and Kits is by keeping calm and trying to remember. OK?'

Lisa nodded.

'I'm seeing a psychologist,' she said, quietly. 'The police set it up. For counselling, you know. They reckon if I can get through the shock, the guilt feelings, something might just come back.'

'Good,' said James. 'That's good. Look are you sure I can't get you a coffee or something? You look dreadful.'

23

'Thanks! You don't look too great yourself.'

'Yeah, well, I haven't slept much since . . .'

'Me neither,' said Lisa, smiling faintly at him as she began to move away. 'Look . . . tell Kits I'm thinking about her, won't you? If you can . . . if it won't upset her.'

Kits was sitting up in bed, when James got back. She looked at her watch. Visiting time was almost over. Mum would stay, of course, as she always did. But the rest of the family had been taking it in turns to visit, so as not to over tire her. James and Lewis had been bullied into going back to their schools and only visiting in the evenings. Grandad Bill and Grandma Helen had been. So had Grandma Joyce. But she hadn't stayed long.

Maybe it had been a mistake to tell her about Grandad, Kits reflected. Grandma Joyce hadn't believed her. Nobody believed her. Poor Grandma had muttered, 'Kits, oh, Kits,' over and over before rushing from the room in tears.

Kits blinked, banishing painful thoughts and mechanically began to stack the Get Well cards which she'd been poring over with Mum and Lewis, as James took up his usual perch on the end of the bed.

'You've been a long time with Lisa, haven't you?' she snapped.

'Sorry,' said James. 'But I couldn't just leave her. She was upset, she . . .'

'Oh, poor thing,' said Kits, almost spitting the words.

'Have you seen this one?' said her mother, hastily grabbing a card. 'From your headmistress. Everyone's been so kind.'

'Wonderful,' said Kits, pushing the card from her mother's hand. 'Feeling sorry for the cripple.'

Lewis stuck his fist in his mouth. This wasn't Kits. This wasn't his sister. Kits was the cheerful one of the family. Always having a joke. Always optimistic. He'd never heard her so bitter and angry before.

'Don't say that,' said Mrs Bellingham, looking at her daughter.

'Well, it's true, isn't it?' said Kits. 'I've seen you all, looking at each other. I've heard you all whispering. Wondering what to tell me. When to tell me. How to tell me. Well, you needn't bother. I've saved you the trouble. I already know. I'm not going to get better. Not properly. I'm never going to walk again, am I?'

James had to speak. His mother was crying. Lewis had slumped into a chair in the corner.

'We don't know that. Not for sure.'

'Maybe you don't. But I do. Look,' she said snatching a pen from the bedside cabinet and stabbing her leg. 'No feeling. There's no feeling. There's nothing there . . .'

James grabbed the pen from her.

'Kits,' he said. 'Kits?'

She was staring blankly ahead, her eyes open unnaturally wide, head tilted slightly back. She neither saw nor heard him.

'Lewis. Get the nurse.'

Mrs Bellingham gently shook Kits' shoulders.

The eyelids dropped. Kits blinked.

'Are they here yet?' she asked.

'Who, love?'

'The police.'

'What do you mean?'

'They're coming to talk to me. About the accident.'

'Well they've been asking to. They're desperate for some sort of lead. Something to go on but the doctor says . . .'

'The doctor's agreed,' said Kits firmly. 'They're coming tonight. Now.'

Lewis came back with the nurse.

'I think she's OK now,' said James, hastily explaining what had happened.

The nurse looked at Kits' eyes and took her pulse.

'Well she seems all right but I'll let Doctor know. Maybe it's still too soon. I'll check with Doctor before I let them in.'

'Who?' said Mrs Bellingham.

'The police. They've just arrived. They were supposed to be coming earlier but got delayed. Didn't Sister tell you?'

'No,' said Mrs Bellingham. 'I mean, I don't think so. But she must have done. Kits knew about it. Perhaps I wasn't listening properly. I've been a bit . . .'

'It's all right,' said the nurse. 'I understand. It's late. You're all tired. Perhaps it's best if they come back tomorrow.'

'No,' said Kits. 'Now. I want to see them now. I want to get it over with.'

The nurse brought two chairs to the side of the bed, as the police officers came in. A man and a lady. They sat down, introduced themselves, explained in hushed voices what they wanted.

'Take your time,' the lady said. 'Just tell us, in your own words, what happened. Right from the beginning.'

'We'd been to netball club after school,' Kits began. 'Like we always do on a Monday. We walk, together, as far as Lisa's and then I get my bus to go home. Lisa's isn't far from the school. You don't have to go round the main road way. You can cut down Freeman's Hill and Slade Lane . . . Look, I'm sure Lisa's told you all this.'

'No,' said the police lady. 'It's not only the accident she doesn't remember. I'm afraid she's got a complete block from the time you left the school. It's common in trauma cases.'

'Trauma,' Kits screamed. 'What's she got to be traumatized about? She's fine, isn't she?'

'Physically, yes. But she can't tell us anything. No other witnesses have come forward, so we're relying on you. If you're up to it.'

'I won't be much help. When I think about it, it's all a blur of mixed-up images – like peering through a thick fog. Outlines, shapes but no details. Nothing you can really focus on. Nothing that would help.'

'Just tell us what you know,' the policeman urged.

'OK,' said Kits, briefly closing her eyes, trying desperately to remember. 'We'd gone down the hill and turned into Slade Lane. There's no pavement or anything but we were being careful. Walking close to the hedge, to the ditch, facing oncoming traffic like you're supposed to. We'd even got those stupid reflective strips on our jackets.'

'Who was on the inside?'

Kits thought for a moment.

'She was. Lisa.'

'Did any cars pass?'

'I don't think so. There'd been a couple. On the hill. But you don't get much round there. I can't be sure though. We were talking. I mean you don't always take in what's going on, do you? You don't think your life's suddenly going to change. That you'll be asked to remember every little detail like some flaming test. It was an ordinary day. Just an ordinary day.'

Kits paused, looking down at her pale fingertips, thinking how ordinary it had been. The usual rows over breakfast. Lewis scurrying around trying to find his football boots. James hurriedly finishing off a bit of homework, as always. Mum burning her toast. Dad yelling at them all for being so disorganized. Mum shouting at Dad for shouting.

Then an ordinary, not to say boring, morning at school. Spending break in the library with Lisa. Helping her to learn her French because there'd been some sort of bother again at home and Lisa hadn't had time. That, followed by the French test and a video in history before lunch.

Sitting in lessons in the afternoon, looking forward to netball. Laughing, at the end of the practice, when she missed a clear shot at goal. Never realizing it was her last chance.

The very last game she would ever play.

CHAPTER THREE

'Are you all right?' Kits heard the policewoman say. 'Do you want to stop?'

'No. I'm OK. I was just thinking. How ordinary everything was. How I did exactly the same things I do every Monday. Me and Lisa were just walking along after netball, talking. She was telling me how her mum had been fussing about her staying on for clubs after school. She's a bit strange like that, is Lisa's mum. A bit neurotic. Very protective.

'Anyway, I remember noticing headlights as the car came towards us. But I didn't think anything of it. The road's quite straight. The driver must have seen us. He must have seen us.'

'He?'

'He, she, I don't know. I didn't look. I didn't have time. It speeded up. I swear it speeded up. It drove straight at us.'

The police officers looked at each other. Looked at Mrs Bellingham.

'Are you sure?' the man said. 'Are you saying you think it was deliberate?'

'It must have been,' said Kits. 'There was plenty of room. No other cars. No reason to swerve. He must have seen us.'

'And the car,' the policeman urged. 'What was it like? Did you recognize . . . ?'

'No,' said Kits. 'No. It was dark. It all happened so quickly. All cars look the same to me. It's not something I notice.'

'That's right,' said Lewis. 'Doesn't know a Jag from a Merc. Uncle Alex had his new car for a month before Kits even noticed. Girls don't, do they?'

The police lady raised her eyes at this blatant piece of sexism but said nothing.

'And I don't suppose you clocked a number,' said the policeman. 'Just one letter or digit would help.'

'No. Nothing. No details. If I'd noticed anything at the time it would be there, now, in my head. But it's not. Just the lights and the sound of the engine drowning Lisa's screams as I pushed . . . oh no . . .'

'What is it?' said Mrs Bellingham, putting her arms round her daughter as she started to cry.

'I pushed her,' sobbed Kits. 'That's how she ended up in the ditch. Safe. I pushed her. I wasn't being a heroine or anything. I saw it coming. I think we both saw it. Realized in the same second. She froze. I tried to get us both out of the way. She made it. I didn't. But she didn't leave me. She didn't jump. I pushed her.'

31

The police officers stood up to leave, realizing that, for the moment, they would get no further.

'What now?' Mrs Bellingham asked them.

'We haven't got much to go on,' said the policeman. 'We're still appealing for witnesses. Checking all the local garages. The car must have sustained some damage. Somebody must know something.'

'But could it have been deliberate?' Mrs Bellingham whispered. 'Like she said. I mean it's hard enough to believe a driver would hit someone and just drive off, let alone do it deliberately . . . I mean what sort of person would . . . ?'

'Hard to say,' said the policeman. 'The driver could have been drunk, drugged, mad or all three. I won't speculate on motive but I will find the person responsible. It it's humanly possible, I'll find him. I promise you that.'

The words were comforting, but only for a moment. Whatever they did, Mrs Bellingham thought as she watched them leave, it wouldn't help Kits to walk again. She turned her attention back to her daughter, sitting down beside her, stroking her hair.

'Are you OK?'

'I've got to see Lisa. I've got to tell her. I want to see her . . .'

'Tomorrow, love,' said Mrs Bellingham. 'It can wait till tomorrow. It's late . . .'

'But I've got to see her. I've got to explain.'

'Lisa understands,' said James. 'She knows what you've been through. She knows you haven't been quite yourself.'

'Not quite myself,' said Kits, laughing bitterly. 'No, I'm not, am I? I'm not ever going to be myself again.'

'Yes you will,' insisted Mrs Bellingham. 'Once you're allowed up . . . you might not be able to walk, at least for a time, but you'll be able to get around. You'll cope, Kits. You always do.'

'You don't understand,' Kits shouted. 'None of you understand. It's not just a physical thing . . . it's in my head. Everything's changed. The way I see things, think things, feel things. Like someone . . . something's taken over. I don't recognize myself. I'm not in control anymore.'

'What sort of things, love?' said Mrs Bellingham, looking anxiously at James and Lewis. 'What do you mean?'

Kits stared hard at them for a moment, wondering what to say, how much to reveal.

'Like what happened tonight,' she said hesitantly. 'I knew those police officers were coming to see me.'

'You must have heard someone mention it,' said her mother.

'Nobody told me. I just knew,' Kits insisted. 'Like I know ten seconds before the nurses come in with my tablets and stuff.'

33

'You've got used to the routine, that's all,' said Mrs Bellingham.

'And when James said I had a visitor, I knew it was Lisa, didn't I? Tell her, James. Tell her about that.'

'It's true,' said James. 'But it wasn't really that hard to guess. Lisa's been phoning or turning up most days.'

'So have loads of other people,' said Kits. 'But I knew it wasn't Auntie Pat or my teacher, didn't I?'

'A lucky . . .'

'Oh, forget it,' Kits snapped. 'I don't know why I bothered. I knew you wouldn't believe me. Just like you didn't believe me about the floating and the lights.'

'The doctor explained all that, Kits,' said James, gently. 'It's called an out-of-body experience. Dozens of patients report similar experiences after ops. Now if you're into mumbo-jumbo X-files stuff, you say the spirit leaves the body. Goes walkabout on its own. Some people even report getting as far as heaven. Seeing God. Well, maybe they do. I don't know. But the more scientific explanation is temporary trauma to the brain. Oxygen shortage. Impact of the anaesthetic, whatever. That's what you experienced, Kits. And of course we believe you. But we also know there's a perfectly rational explanation. It's nothing to worry about.'

'And seeing Grandad? Talking to him. Holding

34

his hand. Rationalize that one,' said Kits.

'Now that one I do understand,' said James. 'It's only been a year since he died. I still have dreams about him. Really vivid dreams. So vivid that I wake up and, for a moment, I think he's there with me.'

'It wasn't a dream!'

'Yes it was, Kits,' said James. 'Heightened by the effect of all the drugs they'd been pumping into you, but still a dream. There's nothing wrong with your mind Kits. Believe me . . .'

'I wish I could,' said Kits. 'But you don't know what it's like. None of you knows.'

Lisa looked anxiously at her watch, as she got off the bus outside the hospital on Saturday afternoon. Almost three o'clock. It had been midday when she'd phoned the hospital. Mrs Bellingham had said Kits wanted to see her. No, not wanted. The word she had used was desperate. Kits was desperate to see her.

'She's remembered something,' Mrs Bellingham had said. 'She wants to tell you herself. I can't get her to settle. We had a dreadful night. You will come, won't you? As soon as possible. I'd pick you up only James has borrowed my car to take Lewis to football. I encourage them to do things as normally as possible . . .'

It was funny, Lisa thought, how everything had

changed. Even Mrs Bellingham's voice was barely recognizable since the accident. The posh, smooth tones had become choked, anxious, neurotic. Transmitting their urgency down the phone line. Lisa had been set to leave almost immediately. But nothing had gone right. She'd got into a row with Mum. Something stupid and petty but it had taken up time, meant she had missed the bus and had to wait over an hour for the next one.

Sixty-five minutes with her stomach churning and her head throbbing. Wanting to see Kits. Not wanting to see Kits. Terrified of what she would find.

She raced along the corridors. Up the stairs, following the signs to the ward. She stopped at the desk.

'Lisa Mountjoy,' she said to the nurse. 'I've come to see Kits . . . Katherine Bellingham.'

'Oh, yes,' said the nurse, indicating the room. 'Mrs Bellingham said they were expecting you. Go in.'

The door was open. Mrs Bellingham stood up to greet her as Lisa hovered, nervously, in the doorway.

'Sorry I'm late,' said Lisa, 'I missed the bus, I . . .'

'That's all right, love,' said Mrs Bellingham. 'Go in. I was just going to fetch some drinks. Coffee?'

Lisa wasn't sure whether she answered or not, as Mrs Bellingham moved, leaving her in full view of Kits.

'Lisa!' Kits called out.

Lisa moved quickly towards the bed, blinking back tears.

'Don't,' Kits warned. 'Please don't, or you'll set me off!'

'I'm sorry,' said Lisa staring at a face, a body, she barely recognized. 'Oh, Kits, I'm so sorry.'

'No,' said Kits. 'Don't say that. It's me that should apologize. If you knew the things I've been thinking. The things I've been saying . . .'

'It's all right,' said Lisa, sinking into a chair, stretching out her hand to Kits.

'No, it's not all right,' said Kits. 'Don't you understand, Lisa? I've been blaming you for what happened.'

'Not as much as I've blamed myself,' said Lisa, quietly. 'I don't know what happened back there but . . .'

'I do,' said Kits. 'I've remembered. I've remembered what happened. I think, deep down, I'd always remembered. I think I always knew. But I've been driven half crazy, Lisa. Lying here, burning with anger, wanting to hurt somebody, wanting to hit back. It was easy to tell myself it was your fault. That you left me. Got out of the way. Saved yourself. But it wasn't like that . . .'

Lisa listened, trying to remember, trying to force herself back there. On that road. With Kits. She tried to see what Kits was seeing. But it was as if

37

Kits was talking about someone else. As if the accident had involved some other Lisa. Not her. Her mind was a total blank.

'I pushed you,' Kits was saying. 'You screamed. It wasn't your fault. There was nothing you could have done.'

'We don't know that,' said Lisa, shaking her head. 'If I'd been concentrating. If I'd been a bit more alert maybe . . .'

'Maybe, if only,' said Kits. 'What's the point? What difference will it make? I've been through all that time and time over. If we hadn't been chatting. If we'd taken longer in the showers, left school a minute later. If we'd walked the long way round for a change. But we didn't. It happened.'

'It happened to you,' said Lisa. 'Not me. Why you, Kits? Why can't I remember?'

'Trauma,' said Kits. 'Shock. Guilt feelings, even. But don't you see, Lisa? This changes everything. Knowing you're not to blame. Knowing there was nothing you could have done. Something might start to come back. It might make all the difference.'

'I hope so,' said Lisa. 'I'd give anything to be able to remember . . . to help the police find that driver . . . but . . .'

'What?' said Kits.

'I don't know,' said Lisa slowly. 'I feel . . . I feel . . . scared, Kits. Almost as if I don't want to remember. As if I'm fighting myself. Whenever I

38

try to think about it, to answer questions, I hear a door slamming. Only it's me that's slamming it. I'm leaning against it with all my weight because I don't want to see what's behind it.'

'But that's crazy,' said Kits, gently.

'Don't say that,' Lisa snapped. 'I'm sorry . . . but having to see that psychologist's made me a bit sensitive about madness and stuff. She's OK but she's into everything. Asking about school. About my family. Making a big deal out of Mum being a single parent. As if it's relevant! I feel worse after therapy than when I started. The whole business makes me feel I'm going out of my mind.'

'I know what you mean,' said Kits.

'And it's not even working. It hasn't brought anything back,' said Lisa. 'Not a thing. I usually end up crying and all she says is I need to relax, let go, get back to school. Start getting back to normal as she puts it. What the hell's normal supposed to be?'

Good question, Kits thought. They'd all changed so much. Since the accident, it seemed as though everybody . . . she, her family, Lisa . . . had been ripped apart like a jigsaw and the pieces thrown roughly back together again. Not one of them fitting properly. Dad's hair had turned visibly greyer. Mum had lost over a stone. James, normally so laid-back and calm, jumped at every little sound. Poor Lewis barely spoke. And as for her! She barely recognized the snapping, snarling creature she'd become.

'I don't know,' she said, trying not to dwell too much on herself. 'But I think it helped Lewis to get back to school. And James says battling with his college work stops him brooding too much . . .'

'Yeah,' said Lisa. 'I'd already sort of decided to go back on Monday. It'll keep me out of Mum's way if nothing else.'

'Trouble again?' said Kits.

'The usual,' said Lisa shrugging.

Kits didn't pry. She had learnt over the months of knowing Lisa that it didn't do any good. You had to let things come out in their own time and their own way. If you asked too many questions Lisa simply retreated into her shell.

Lisa hardly ever talked about her family. It had been hard enough getting her to talk about anything at first. Now she'd chat about school, films, music, ordinary stuff but rarely about her home life. All Kits really knew was that she lived with her mum and twin brothers who were much younger than Lisa. Kits had never met them. No-one from school was ever invited to Lisa's house. There had never been any mention of a dad or grandparents or aunts and uncles or even family friends.

Sometimes when Lisa was obviously upset, she would talk about the rows. According to Lisa the usual meant rows about clothes, make-up, boys and staying out late. But you couldn't help thinking it was more than that. Those sorts of things didn't make you hate a parent, the way Lisa seemed to hate her mum sometimes.

'Anyway,' Lisa was saying. 'What about you? Everyone's bound to be asking. Have the doctors said when you'll be able to go back?'

Kits looked down at the bed.

'I know it will be a long time,' said Lisa. 'I just wondered if you had any idea at all. I mean would Easter be too optimistic?'

'Maybe before then, if I'm lucky, but . . .'

'What?' said Lisa.

'It won't be my old school . . . your school,' said Kits, watching Lisa's face crumple. 'There aren't the facilities. I'll be in a wheelchair. It's the wrong sort of building entirely. Dad's been onto the Education Authority. The nearest school with ramps and stuff is Stangate.'

'But that's miles away.'

'There's a special bus . . . for people with . . . disabilities. I'm dreading it, Lisa,' Kits confessed. 'It's going to be awful.'

'It'll be fine,' said Lisa, trying to smile. Trying to be brave, for Kits' sake. 'You're brilliant enough to get on anywhere . . . you'll make new friends.'

Kits heard the words clearly enough but with the words came a feeling. No, not one. An over-powering confusion of feelings. Fear, loss, isolation,

41

anger, frustration, self-pity, guilt. An ordinary enough tangle of emotions given the circumstances. So commonplace in recent days that it took Kits a moment to realize what was wrong. These weren't her feelings. They were alien emotions, invading from the outside, seeping through every pore. These were Lisa's feelings. They were coming from Lisa.

CHAPTER FOUR

'You've missed the turning,' Kits said.

Her dad looked at the map as Mrs Bellingham slowed down and prepared to stop.

'No, I don't think so,' Mr Bellingham said.

'You have,' Kits insisted.

She shivered as her mum prepared to reverse. She knew she was right but she didn't know how she knew. She had never been here before. At least, she didn't think so. But, somehow, she knew the landscape as clearly as she knew her own street.

Maybe she should have kept quiet. Delayed their arrival for a bit longer. But that's all it would have been. A delay. Best to get it over with.

She didn't feel ready to go back to school. Not this school. A strange school. Stangate. But her physiotherapist, who came three times a week, had insisted she ought to try.

Try! As if she hadn't been trying! Doing all the stupid exercises. The pushing, the pulling, the special breathing. And for what? Nothing. She still couldn't walk. Wouldn't ever walk.

'Just round the corner and under a bridge,' Kits muttered as her mother slowed down and hesitated.

'That's the school sign,' said Mr Bellingham, turning round, staring at Kits quizzically, as they passed under the bridge.

'I told you,' she said and then wished she hadn't.

Her parents would talk about it later, in hushed voices, the way they talked about everything now. Analysing her every word, the slightest movement, any tiny stupid thing she managed to do for herself. Looking for signs of progress . . . or regression.

This visit, she imagined, would count as progress. Getting her as far as the school, for a preliminary visit, to have a look round, to see if she liked it.

Not that it would make any difference. It wasn't as though she had a choice. It wasn't every school that could cope with wheelchairs.

She cringed as she saw her dad getting the hated object out of the boot and setting it up. She squirmed as he lifted her, then flopped back in the chair, her arms dangling.

There was no way she was going to propel herself. If they wanted her to go up that ramp and through the main doors, they would have to push her.

Kits thought she saw a hint of a frown from the woman who was waiting to greet them.

She wanted to shout out.

'OK . . . so maybe I could do it myself. Maybe I

should. But I'm not going to. And do you know why? Because I don't flaming want to. I don't want to use my arms. I want to use my legs. I want to walk.'

The woman introduced herself as Mrs Hewitt, headmistress, and took them into her office where she wrote down a few details before beginning the grand tour. It was a modern school, she crowed, purpose-built.

She was so pathetically proud of it, Kits thought. The extra space in the classrooms, the ramps, the wide corridors, the lifts with buttons low down. Big flaming deal!

Not that all the pupils needed those little extras. Not all of them were disabled. It wasn't a special school in that sense. The key, the headmistress gushingly pointed out, was integration. Normality. With extra help, extra staff, extra facilities for those who needed it.

Was it her imagination, Kits wondered, or did Mrs Hewitt derive some sadistic pleasure from pointing out the glorious range of disabilities they catered for? The notices posted in Braille, for the partially sighted, the computer programs for the dyslexic and the special gadgets in the loos which allowed all but the most severely disabled to go in private.

Mrs Hewitt pretended to be oh so politically correct, never mentioning emotive words like blind, deaf or paralysed. So why was it that all the pupils she stopped to talk to on their tour were the disabled ones? Never the fully functional ones. What sort of point did she think she was making?

'We have someone in our assemblies who does sign language translations,' the head was droning on. 'And what Katherine might be particularly interested in, is our swimming pool. A specialist comes three mornings a week to . . .'

'Play with the cripples,' said Kits.

'Kits, please . . . ,' said Mrs Bellingham, hastily apologizing to the headmistress.

'It's all right,' she simpered. 'It takes a while but we find most of our pupils settle.'

She nodded at a boy who was racing down an intersecting corridor in a wheelchair.

'Paul had a terrible accident on a skiing trip with his old school. It was a dreadful blow. He was such an active boy. Really talented footballer. It was hard for him to accept at first but now he's into everything. He plays tennis, swims . . . I believe you like sport, Katherine?'

'Proper sports,' said Kits, bitterly. 'I like proper sports. Where you move. Run around. Jump. Not sports for mutants crashing around in wheelchairs.'

Kits was exhausted when they got home. It hadn't been an enormous success and exertion of any sort still tired her. Dad had gone back into work for a couple of hours. Mum was pottering around. Keeping busy. Keeping her mind off things.

Kits dozed for a while and then shouted to her mum to put a video on. The programme had just ended when Lewis came home.

'Turn it off,' said Kits.

She'd discovered she didn't have to bother saying please and thank you anymore.

'What was it like? . . . The school,' Lewis added as Kits failed to answer.

'A freak show. That's what it was like.'

'Oh . . . I thought . . .'

'Amazing,' said Kits. 'And I always imagined you had to have a brain to think.'

'I'm sorry . . .'

'Don't be. Some of us have legs. Some of us have brains. Go kick a football around. Stick to what you're good at.'

Lewis crashed into James on his way out.

'Oh, Lew, not again,' said James, catching hold of him. 'You've got to stop this. You've got to stop crying over every little thing she says to you . . .'

'They're not little things,' said Lewis. 'Not jokes, like before. She's so . . . so . . . sometimes I think she hates me.'

'No.'

'She does!' said Lewis, pulling away. 'She hates all of us.'

James shrugged and went into Kits' room, the downstairs room, which they'd converted to a bedroom and where Kits spent most of her time now.

'Hi, Kits,' he said.

He avoided the mistake Lewis had made. He wasn't going to ask about the school.

'Can you give us a hand with this chart thing I've got to do for college?'

'Hands, I can do,' said Kits, trying to be more pleasant than she'd been with Lewis. 'Oh, for goodness' sake, James. You've got it all mixed up, as usual. Get me an eraser.'

James dumped the work on the tray attached to her wheelchair and went off in search of the eraser. Kits picked up a pencil to start the alterations but it slipped from her grasp, slid down the side of her chair and onto the floor.

'Mum!' she screamed. 'Mum!'

No-one came. Sometimes they didn't. Mainly they did, as soon as she shouted out, but sometimes they didn't hear. It was an old house with thick walls. Sometimes you just had to wait.

She stared at the pencil. It was only a few centimetres away. In the old days she'd only have had to reach out. Take a small step.

'One small step for mankind,' she muttered. 'And a total bloody impossibility for me.'

She stared at the pencil again. Hating it. Hating

48

it for reminding her. Hating it for sitting there, mocking her. Challenging her. Daring her to pick it up.

She'd move it. She'd make it move. It wasn't going to defy her like that. It wasn't going to get away with it.

She imagined it rising up. Coming towards her. Thought of its frail, inanimate thinness. She was stronger by far. It would move. She would make it move.

Thought gave way to sheer force of will. Her whole mind, her total energy focused on having the pencil in her grasp.

Her body felt it, before her eyes saw. It was moving. Really moving. Hovering just above the carpet. Not far. Not far enough. But it would be. It was coming. Slowly. Slowly.

It dropped to the floor as the door opened, breaking her grip, shattering her concentration.

'Got it,' said James, putting the eraser on the tray. 'Whoops, pencil's on the floor.'

He bent down, picked it up and gave it to her.

'You spoilt it,' Kits yelled, snapping the pencil into four pieces. 'I had it. I was doing it and you spoilt it.'

She shoved his work into his hands.

'Get out. Do it yourself.'

'Kits, I . . . what's wrong . . . don't you feel well . . . can I . . . ?'

Suddenly she was crying. James knelt down, beside her.

'I'm sorry,' she said. 'I'm sorry. It's been a bad day. I'm tired. And then . . . the things I see, the things in my head . . . it's getting worse, James.'

James didn't want to ask. He knew. They all knew the sort of things Kit had seen or done since the accident. It was weird. Creepy. He didn't want to admit it to anyone but it scared him.

'I saw it move. The pencil. I made it move. With my mind. But I couldn't have done, could I? I imagined it because I want to do things. Go places. On my own. I want to be me again, James.'

He was saved from saying anything by the appearance of Lewis at the door.

'Have you got the key to the bike shed, James? I'm going out for a bit.'

James stood up and took the key from his pocket. Kits stared hard at Lewis, blinked, stared again.

'No,' she said. 'Don't.'

'Don't what?'

'Don't give him the key. He's not to go out on his bike.'

'Kits, don't be silly,' said James, giving the key to his brother. 'You can't stop people doing things just because . . .'

'It's all right,' said Lewis. 'I don't need to. It doesn't matter.'

'Yes it does,' said James, pushing him out. 'Go.'
James turned to Kits.

'This has got to stop, Kits,' he said. 'I'm sorry.
We're all sorry about what happened. But we can't
go on like this, pandering to your every whim. Not
for ever. You've got to get a grip. You've got to try,
Kits. It's ruining our lives. All our lives. Your life.'

'You don't understand.'

'Yes I do. I try. We all try. I don't know what
you want anymore, Kits. If we feel sorry for you
it's wrong. If we try to get you to do things, it's
wrong. If we stay in, it's wrong. If we go out
it's wrong. Lewis was right. You're starting to hate
us, Kits. You hate us for being able to do the things
you can't anymore. And do you know what's
worse? You're starting to hate yourself, too. That's
what I can't stand. I can't stand watching you do
that.'

'You're wrong,' Kits screamed at him. 'You
don't understand. The bike isn't safe . . . I can feel
it . . . I just know.'

James opened his mouth to speak and closed
it again. This could be hysteria. Kits trying to
manipulate them. She'd had enough practice
recently! But on the other hand . . . if she was right
. . . like she'd been right about things before. If
anything happened to Lewis . . .

'OK,' he said. 'I'll go out. I'll find him. I'll check
the bike over. Will that make you happy?'

51

Kits nodded.

Her head flopped back as he went out. What was happening to her? Where did these ideas, these feelings come from? She'd had so many of them recently. More than when she'd been in hospital. Stupid, petty things mostly, like knowing the instant someone was about to walk through the door. Knowing exactly what they were going to say. Not all the time. But some of the time. Enough of the time to make you think . . . to make you think you were going mad.

She ran her tongue round her mouth. It was dry. Her throat was dry. She needed a drink. There was a glass of orange on the bedside table. She pushed herself towards it. Drat. Mum had left a chair in the way, when she'd been cleaning up, earlier. She'd have to shout.

But instead of shouting, she stared at the glass. If she could move pencils, if she hadn't imagined it, it was worth a try. She was thirsty. Very thirsty. She concentrated hard on the thirst. On the need for that glass.

It was easy, really. Like floating. She still floated sometimes. At night. On her own. When the house was quiet. She hadn't told anybody, of course. Not after how worried they'd been the first time. It was her secret. Her secret power. And now she had another one.

She stretched out her hand, as the glass moved

towards her. Closed her fingers around it. Lifted it to her lips. Finished off the juice. She put the glass down on her tray and looked around the room.

Picture. How about lifting the picture off the wall? That would be fun.

CHAPTER FIVE

James came back and sat at the kitchen table, staring at his work.

'You've been a long time. Did you find him?' his mother asked.

'Yeah. He was riding his bike up and down the towpath.'

'The towpath! He knows I don't like him going there. It's getting dark and . . .'

'Mum! Stop worrying. He's on the section parallel to the road. It's plenty light enough. He's with his friends. I've checked the bike. All the lights are functioning. But one of the tyres was a bit flat. I've sorted it. To keep Kits off my back. Stupid really. It would have been fine. But . . .'

'You sound as though you're starting to believe . . .'

'No. Not really.'

'Good. You, of all people, should have more sense. Lewis, I can understand. All those *Goosebumps* books he reads. And the stuff I catch him watching on telly! Add that to the strain we've all been under. Even your dad was talking about telling the doctor. Asking for another brain scan. As if Kits being paralysed wasn't enough . . . we've got to start imagining brain damage as well.'

'Dad doesn't think of it as damage . . . as such . . .'

'There's nothing to think about,' Mrs Bellingham insisted. 'People see what they want to see. The more you believe in something, the more proof you find. It's like horoscopes. If you're convinced you're a typical Leo, you'll find the evidence to prove it. Now, come on. Get that work done. I want to wipe the table. Lisa's coming round soon and I don't want the place in a mess.'

'She's coming to see Kits, not to inspect the cleaning!'

'Yes but you know I don't like . . .'

The crash prevented her finishing her sentence. She and James both raced to Kits' room. Stood at the doorway. Breathed audible sighs of relief. She was fine. It took them a moment to discover the cause of the crash. A picture had fallen off the wall. The frame was broken. Glass littered the carpet.

Mrs Bellingham scurried off to get a brush. James went and examined the picture frame.

'How on earth did that happen?'

Kits smiled, placidly. She wasn't going to tell him. She wasn't going to tell them anything else. Dad and Lewis were already getting edgy. They didn't understand. This was her compensation. Her little consolation prize. OK, so she couldn't walk but she could do other things. Once she'd learnt to do them properly – to control them . . . But they had to be secret. She knew that. Any hint of what she was doing and they'd have her dragged off to the psychologist.

So far she'd resisted all attempts at counselling. Partly because she didn't need it and partly because she'd learnt enough from Lisa to know she wouldn't like it.

'Stop mucking with it, James. You'll have the hook out of the wall next.'

'But I can't figure out . . .'

'Dad put the picture up, right?' said Kits. 'When I moved in here?'

James laughed. Enough said. Dad had many talents but DIY wasn't amongst them.

When Mum returned, Lisa was with her. Prompt, as ever, for her weekly visit.

'Are you OK?' Kits asked.

Strange question, James thought. Lisa looked fine to him. Better than she'd done for weeks now. She was very attractive with all that dark hair and brown eyes which flickered, timidly, under thick, dark lashes. But he'd only really begun to notice her properly, as a person, since the accident. They talked more now. Lisa had lost some of her reserve. Their shared concern for Kits had brought them closer.

'Yeah,' Lisa was saying. 'Had a bit of bother at home, before I came out. The twins were playing up because Mum wouldn't let them go out. Not even in the garden. Honestly it's like a prison camp. Mum's worse than ever since the . . .'

'Accident,' Kits said for her.

'Yeah. Well, Liam was screaming, Toby was crying and then Mum rounded on me, asking why I was going out again. She hates me going anywhere. Especially at night. Wants me in by nine. It's like the flaming Inquisition. Where am I going? Who am I seeing? When will I be back?'

Mrs Bellingham raised her eyebrows, finished clearing up and left them to it. She felt sympathy for Lisa's mum but, on the other hand, you couldn't lock your children up in order to protect them. Goodness knows, they'd always been careful. Kits was never allowed out late unless someone went and picked her up. They'd tortured themselves since the accident, agonizing over whether they should have let her walk back from school after sport fixtures.

In the end you had to accept that it wasn't your fault. Tragedy could strike any time, night or day, even when you though your kids were really safe. She'd just heard about another shooting in a school in America. She shuddered. What made people do things like that? What kind of maniacs were they? The kind who'd knocked Kits over and then driven off? He could have killed her. She could have died back there, on that road. She wasn't dead and they had to be thankful for that but . . .

She tipped the broken glass onto some newspaper. Wrapped it up. Threw it away. Wiped over some surfaces she'd cleaned earlier. Keep busy. Keep busy. It was the only way . . .

Lisa sat on the chair next to Kits' bed. James had settled in the corner with a book but she guessed he wasn't reading it. He often hovered, when she came to see Kits. Joining in sometimes with the conversation, but mainly blending into the background.

She was glad when he stayed. It reassured her to have someone else in the room, in case Kits got worked up. You had to be so careful, these days, not to say the wrong thing, or even to think it. Kits seemed to pick up on everything.

Last week it had been netball. Lisa had been wondering whether to tell Kits that the team had made it to the semi-finals. Just that. Just wondering. And Kits had suddenly got all agitated, throwing her head back, as if she was having some sort of fit.

'Don't,' she'd screamed at Lisa. 'I can't bear it. I can't bear to think about it.'

Lisa shook her head, clearing away her thoughts, trying to grasp onto something that was safe to talk about.

'I'm starting my new school, next week,' Kits volunteered.

'You went to see it today, didn't you?'

'Yeah. That's why I'm a bit floppy. Give me a nudge if I start falling asleep.'

'Dare I ask?'

'It was OK. I suppose.'

Lisa smiled, trying to be brave, for Kits' sake.

'I'll miss you, though,' Kits added.

'I know,' said Lisa. 'I miss you too. School's just not the same anymore. You know, I even thought of getting a transfer to Stangate myself.'

'Could you do that?' said Kits, suddenly animated. 'Would they let you?'

'In theory, yes. I talked to Mr Potter, at school, about it first. He thought I was being a bit stupid. You know. They always tell you you'll make new friends, don't they? Anyway, he made enquiries and even talked to my mum for me. But she won't have it. Says I've been to too many schools already. I mean, whose fault's that? It's her that keeps insisting on moving all the time. And then she started moaning about the expense. New uniform and we'd probably have to pay for transport.'

'Why? We don't.'

'That's because you have to go there,' said Lisa. 'Because of the facilities. But I don't. So Mum reckons we'd have to pay, even though she's on income support and stuff. She says there's no way we can afford it.'

Lisa's mum was probably right, Kits thought. Unemployed single parent, three kids . . . it couldn't be easy.

'Have you?' said Kits, as Lisa suddenly announced she'd stopped seeing the psychologist.

'Have I what?' said Lisa.

'Stopped seeing the psychologist? You just said . . .'

Too late, Kits realized Lisa hadn't announced anything at all. Nothing had been said. She'd heard it, like she heard and saw so many things now, but it hadn't been spoken.

'Oh, yes,' said Lisa, playing along, as she'd learnt to do. Pretending that nothing was wrong. That it was perfectly normal for people to respond to your thoughts. 'Yes. Yes I have.'

'Why?' said James, looking up from his book.

'It was no good,' said Lisa. 'I hated going. All that probing was upsetting me. Not just about the accident either. I mean she was really sweet. Got you feeling all cosy and secure. Made out we were playing games all the time. But we weren't. Before you knew where you were she'd have you talking about stuff . . . stuff I don't like talking about. The past. When my brothers were babies . . . what happened to . . . Anyway it had nothing to do with the accident. Nothing. It wasn't helping. I wasn't remembering anything. I kept telling her. I couldn't remember anything. I couldn't. I couldn't.'

James stood up. Lisa's voice was becoming shrill. Hysterical. But it wasn't her he was worried about. It was Kits. Her eyes had started to roll up to the eyelids. Her head flopped back.

'Oh, no,' said Lisa. 'I've upset her, again. I shouldn't have . . .'

'I'll get Mum.'

By the time James came back with his mother, it was over. Just as it had been that time at the hospital. Kits was sitting up, quite normally, staring at Lisa.

'Why?' Kits said.

'Why what?' said Lisa, looking anxiously from James to his mother.

'Why are you doing this?' Kits asked. 'Why are you lying?'

'Lying?' said Lisa, feeling her face burn in confusion. 'What about? What do you mean?'

'Don't play the innocent,' Kits snapped. 'You can't hide it. Not from me. Not now. You've remembered something, haven't you?'

'No,' Lisa protested.

'You have,' Kits insisted. 'It was there. Right at the front of your mind. I saw it. Felt it. Not clearly. I nearly had it but you blocked it. Shut it off.'

'No,' Lisa said again. 'I haven't . . .'

'Now, wait a minute,' Mrs Bellingham interrupted, going over to Kits. 'Calm down, Kits. Think what you're doing. What you're saying. You're claiming that Lisa's withholding some vital information about the accident.'

'Dead right, she is.'

'And you know this because you read her mind?' said Mrs Bellingham, incredulously. 'But that's ridiculous. You must see, Kits . . .'

'Don't look at me,' Kits shouted. 'Look at her. Look at her. Then you'll know.'

Mrs Bellingham turned to Lisa.

'It's not true,' said Lisa.

'I know, love,' said Mrs Bellingham, trying a reassuring smile.

'Kits,' said Lisa, appealing directly to her. 'You can't really believe that. You can't. I'd do anything, Kits. Anything to help find that driver. If I knew anything, if I remembered the tiniest little thing, I'd be down that police station like a shot. Honestly, Kits, I'd let them cut my brain open to get the information if I thought it was there. But it isn't. It's like a programme wiped clean off a tape. It's not there. You can't ever see it again.'

'It's there all right,' said Kits. 'You've just hidden it. For whatever selfish reasons, you've hidden it. But that's fine, isn't it? It's not you that's stuck in a wheelchair for the rest of your life, is it? Always wondering which nutter did this to you and why? It doesn't matter to you, does it?'

Lisa's scream ripped through the room as she rushed out, followed by James. He caught up with her in the kitchen, grabbed both her arms, held her tight, to stop the shaking and the tears.

'I'm sorry,' said James, when she eventually started to calm down. 'I don't know what's happening to Kits. None of us do. She's like this all the time now. Claiming to know things, see things. I know it's hard but try not to take it personally. She's like that with all of us. The whole house is going crazy.'

'But what if she's right?' said Lisa. 'What if I really do know something? What if I am blocking it?'

'Why would you do that?' said James. 'It doesn't make any sense. Like most of Kits' claims. OK, so she's been right about a few, silly things but most of it's just wild guesswork. Neurosis. I mean, before you turned up, she had a go at Lew. Didn't want him to go out. Said his bike wasn't safe. It's a sort of jealousy, see . . .'

'No, I don't see,' said Lisa. 'Kits isn't capable of jealousy!'

'Maybe not before,' said James. 'And don't get me wrong. I'm not criticizing her. It's understandable. She sees us all walking around, riding bikes, getting on with life, whatever . . . and she can't bear it. She tries to stop us in whatever crazy way she can.'

Lisa shook her head, but was prevented from speaking by the sound of the doorbell, long and persistent.

'Drat! That's Dad, forgot his key again,' said James as he flung open the door.

But it wasn't his dad who stood there. It was two young boys. And between them they held a broken bike. Lewis's bike.

'Close your mouth, James,' said Lewis, pushing in between his two friends. 'I'm fine.'

'You don't look fine,' said James, watching water ooze from every item of Lewis's clothing. 'And you smell like a drain clogged up with dead rats.'

'He fell in't canal,' said one of the friends.

'No, I didn't,' said Lewis. 'Not exactly. We were racing along the towpath. I hit a stone. My bike slid down the bank. I went to get it and just slithered in. I was out again in a second.'

'Well get upstairs. Have a shower. Get changed,' said James, urgently. 'Mum'll do her nut, if she sees you like that.'

James thanked Lewis's friends, closed the door and watched Lewis squelching upstairs before turning to Lisa, who was standing absolutely still and deathly white.

'She said the bike wasn't safe, didn't she?' Lisa breathed.

'Lisa!' said James, quietly. 'Don't make this any worse than it is. It's coincidence, that's all. Life isn't

64

safe! Accidents happen all the time. Major accidents. Small accidents. Lewis comes home grazed and bruised all the time. Bikes, skateboards, walls . . . if it's there, Lewis will fall off it!'

'But she *knew*.'

'Auto-suggestion,' said James, grasping at rational explanations.

'I'm not sure what that is,' said Lisa.

'Someone puts an idea in your head,' James explained. 'You think about it. It festers. You end up doing exactly what was suggested to you. Like witch doctors. They let it be known they're sticking a pin in a doll's head and hey presto, person gets nasty headache.'

'So you mean Lewis was thinking about Kits saying the bike wasn't safe and deliberately hit a stone to buckle the wheel and make it come true?'

'Not deliberately,' said James, aware of how feeble it sounded. 'Sort of subconsciously. Or it could have been pure bad luck. Either way . . .'

'Either way,' repeated Lisa, 'she was right. But she can't be right about me, can she, James? I can't be hiding anything, can I? I wouldn't do that to Kits. I couldn't. It just isn't possible.'

CHAPTER SIX

'James,' said Lewis. 'Have you moved my baseball cap?'

'No, why should I have?'

'You haven't borrowed it?'

'I wouldn't be seen dead in your baseball cap, even if it would fit, which it wouldn't.'

'And my football scarf. That's gone too.'

'Oh, for goodness' sake, Lewis,' said Mrs Bellingham. 'I'm surprised you can find anything, the state you leave your things in. You've probably left them at school.'

'No, I haven't. I hung them up. Last night.'

'Well, if you did,' said Mr Bellingham, 'it'll be the first time ever.'

'Try the cupboard, under the stairs,' said Kits.

'And hurry up,' said their mother. 'You haven't even packed your games stuff yet.'

Kits smiled to herself as Lewis slouched off. The chaos was mildly entertaining. A little diversion to stop her thinking too deeply about Lisa, or the failure of the police to trace that car, or the prospect of her second week at that awful school, or the million and one other troubles which plagued her.

'I'm sure we've got a ghost,' Lewis wailed as he dumped his scarf and cap on the table. 'I found them at the back of the cupboard.

'Where you stuffed them last night probably,' said his mother.

'But it's not just that,' Lewis insisted. 'It's other stuff too. Your car keys at the weekend. Dad's briefcase. James's watch.'

'Lewis,' his mother snapped. 'Since when have we needed a ghost to help us lose things?'

'And the doors,' Lewis muttered.

'Now I refuse to believe we've lost any doors,' said Mr Bellingham. 'I'd have noticed.'

'Doors slamming!' said Lewis. 'On their own. When nobody's gone through them.'

'Lewis, please stop being ridiculous. Kits' minibus is here.'

Kits tried to stop herself laughing as she left. Maybe she'd have to be a bit more careful with her experiments, her little games. That's all they were. Games. Moving things. Hiding things. Using the power of her mind. Just for fun. Just to see if she could. Nothing too malicious. Nothing that was going to cause any real bother. She had to have something to amuse herself, didn't she? Some sort of hobby. What else could you do, stuck in a wheel-chair, for the rest of your life? Read. Listen to music. Watch TV. Brood. Feel the anger swelling up inside you, threatening to explode.

She sat, grimly staring out of the window, as the minibus headed off to pick up its last passenger. Following the route it took every day. Along Slade Lane. Past the very place where the accident happened.

Every day, Kits focused all her attention on the spot, hoping to see something, hear something, sense something about the car and its driver.

Each day she'd been disappointed. Since the accident her senses had definitely sharpened. Grown in some way. Maybe she'd developed the mysterious sixth sense that witches and animals were supposed to have. But whatever it was, it was unpredictable. It didn't work all the time. Sometimes she knew what was about to happen, sometimes she didn't. Sometimes she could move objects easily, at other times they fell. The crazy thing – the really crazy thing – was that the more she wanted something, the harder it was to do.

They had already come to the end of Slade Lane. Nothing. What was the point of having these new gifts if she couldn't use them for the only thing that really mattered now? Tracing that driver. Finding out why he did what he did. Making him pay.

Lisa. Her mind returned to Lisa, as it did every day, at this point in the journey. Lisa somehow held the key. Lisa had seen something on the day of the accident. She knew something. But what? And why was she hiding it?

Kits put a thumb up to her mouth, nibbling her nail in frustration. Why had she been so stupid? Why had she blurted out her suspicions like that? Accusing Lisa of lying, outright in front of James and Mum, without a scrap of real evidence to go on? Result: Mum had been furious, James irritatingly over anxious and Lisa scared off. Not surprisingly perhaps, she hadn't been round since, though apparently she still phoned sometimes, pretending to be concerned.

Kits' thoughts were disturbed as the mini-bus stopped and the doors slid open. Paul's chair was wheeled up the ramp and fixed in position next to hers. They were the only two wheelchair cases on this route. Of the other four passengers, two were partially sighted, one had a hearing aid and the other looked perfectly normal, with no outwardly damaged bits.

She didn't know why the normal-looking one qualified for the special bus to Stangate. She didn't ask. She rarely spoke, in fact, and they had all learnt to leave her alone. All but Paul. He usually insisted on chatting whether she bothered to answer him or not.

'Don't suppose you saw the match, last night, did you?' he began.

'My brother had it on,' said Kits. ''Fraid I'm not much interested.'

'You don't like sport, then?'

'Not much point, now, is there? I was never keen on football though. Not since I was nine and they turned me down for the junior school team. I was much better than most of the lads.'

'I thought they weren't allowed to discriminate.'

'Don't you believe it.'

'I used to play,' said Paul. 'But I've taken up swimming now. They reckon it helps to get the strength back. Haven't seen you in the pool.'

'No.'

'You ought to try it. It . . .'

'Has the headmistress recruited you then?'

'What?' said Paul.

'Her campaign to get me to the pool and the gym.'

'No I just thought . . .'

'Well don't. I've got enough people on at me. OK?'

She turned her head away. She didn't want to see the hurt look on his face again. The look that had been there yesterday, when she'd snapped at him. The look she had seen on so many faces recently.

She had tried to stop. She really had. But the minute anybody mentioned anything that reminded her of her disability she was off, snapping and snarling like a rabid bulldog.

Other people seemed to handle it far better than her. Paul, for instance. He'd told her about his skiing accident, with not a trace of bitterness. Joked about it even. But then, his was a genuine accident, not something some nutter had done deliberately. Maybe that helped. And then again, his condition wasn't permanent. Or so he believed. He was going to walk again. He was confident of that.

Her condition wasn't necessarily permanent either. Or so the doctors and physiotherapist kept telling her. With time and effort, she might be able to get around with the aid of a crutch or maybe two. Big deal! There'd been hints that she wasn't trying.

'Hey,' said Paul. 'I'm sorry.'

She realized tears had begun to form in her eyes.

She turned to him to apologize. To tell him it wasn't his fault.

He was really quite attractive, even with that frown. He had deep brown eyes and soft, dark hair, that curled at the nape of his neck. She shook her head. What on earth was she thinking about?

She'd never been too interested in boys. Not in a romantic sense. She had loads of male friends. Several had asked her out but she'd never bothered. She'd always assumed that there would be plenty of time for serious relationships. But there wasn't. Time had run out. No boy in his right mind would fancy her, now. And there was no way she was going to encourage a fellow cripple.

Paul looked at her and smiled. Kits turned away.

She had dismissed Paul from her mind. He was a year older than her. In a different class. On Tuesdays he didn't travel home in the bus. He went to swimming club and his dad collected him later.

She was only thinking about him now, she told herself, because it was gone midnight, she couldn't sleep and had exhausted all other possible subjects.

Sleep was a major problem these days. Her mum said it was because she had no physical exercise, none of the things that used to tire her. Dad tried to make out it was a good sign. That she was coping with school, with a semi-normal existence, without the exhaustion she'd felt in the early weeks following the accident.

She rolled over and looked at the table by the side of the bed. A sleeping pill. The doctor had said it was OK, if she was desperate, but Kits didn't like taking them. Besides, she wasn't quite desperate yet. There was one other possibility. One way of tiring herself.

Floating. Floating made you feel light and sleepy and relaxed. She hadn't done it for a while, though. At first it had been OK. Good fun. Harmless.

But the last time . . . the last time hadn't been so relaxing. She'd had an accident. Ended up on the bedroom floor screaming for help. It had put her off.

She closed her eyes, wondering if she could still do it. At first nothing happened.

'It'll be all right,' she told herself. 'Relax. Relax.'

Slowly she began to rise from the bed. She didn't look down. That was the scary bit. Seeing your own body lying there in bed. It wasn't so bad seeing other people. She floated out, down the corridor, to take a look at Lewis. He was sleeping, all curled up, barely visible under the duvet.

If she wasn't careful, she'd turn into some sort of Peeping Tom. That's what had scared her last time. She'd somehow drifted out into the street. Into a neighbour's house. Seen . . . well, it didn't bear thinking about! She'd been so eager to get out, get home, that she'd made a bit of a crash landing, catapulting herself right out of bed.

She wouldn't make that mistake again. She'd be fine, as long as she stayed in the house. Not that it was easy. Like floating about, weightless, in space, she imagined. Your body – or whatever it was, drifting . . . aimlessly . . . out of the . . .

No. She tried to stop it. Tried to pull back. But it wasn't working. She was drifting down the street. Across the back. Further than she'd been before. She could see the canal. Rows of houses beyond. More behind . . . rows and rows . . .

How did you stop? What if she couldn't get back? How did you stop yourself floating, drifting ... through walls ... one wall ... into a house ... large house ... Not a house exactly. It didn't have the feel of a home, somehow. More like a small hospital. School. Institution of some kind. She couldn't tell. Didn't want to know. She didn't want to be here ... in the dark ... gazing down on faint outlines of furniture ... stairs ... bedrooms. Dozens of bedrooms. Long corridors. A funny bleeping sound, ringing in her ears. And the smell. The smell was bothering her. Reminding her of November 5th. Bonfires. Smoke. Burning. Something was burning. Downstairs. It was coming from downstairs. Like the bleeping sound. Smoke alarm? That no-one but herself could hear. Everyone was asleep.

Not quite everyone. Suddenly two uniformed figures appeared in the corridor, rushing towards the stairs. The next minute she heard the screams, the fire alarm, more screams, confused wails as people awoke to the noise and cried out. She tried to cry out herself but couldn't. Because she wasn't really there. Not in body, anyway.

She was powerless. Totally powerless. She could only watch figures scurrying about. Other figures moving more slowly. Very slowly. Why weren't they hurrying? Didn't they know? Couldn't they hear? Didn't they see?

In an instant, it hit her. They couldn't move. Couldn't see. Couldn't hear. She'd been right. It was some sort of institution. These people were disabled. Not all of them. Some were being assisted by the able-bodied. But there were too many to help. They wouldn't get them all out. They'd never get them all out. They'd be suffocated, burnt. They couldn't help themselves. They were going to die in there. And she was trapped, without a body. Helpless. Condemned to watch them die.

No. She couldn't. Wouldn't. She wasn't here. It wasn't real. Dream. Nightmare. Not true. Not real. She was Kits. Lying in her bed at home. Not here. Not real. Got to get away. Get back. Couldn't help. Couldn't do anything.

'Don't make me stay! Don't make me stay! Don't make me stay!'

'Kits? Kits?' Lewis screamed at her. 'Are you all right? Mum! Dad! James! Come down. Quick.'

James was the last to race downstairs into Kits' bedroom. His father was already lifting her back onto the bed.

'I heard her screaming,' said Lewis, throwing himself at James. 'She was writhing around on the floor. Screaming. Like last time. I was scared.'

'It's all right now,' said James, steering Lewis back towards Kits' bed. 'Now sssh, you don't want to make it any worse. She's calming down.'

Calm was an understatement. Kits lay totally still. Limbs rigid. Eyes rolled back.

'Call the doctor, James,' his mother ordered.

'It's two o'clock in the mor . . .'

'I don't care what time it is, James, just do it.'

CHAPTER SEVEN

Mrs Bellingham was sitting at the kitchen table, head slumped in her hands, when James came back from college.

'How is she?' he asked.

'Kits is fine,' she said, looking up. 'No, don't go through. She's just drifted off to sleep again.'

'Shall I make you a coffee?'

His mother nodded.

'Do I look as bad as I feel?'

'You look awful,' said James. 'But it's hardly surprising. You were up all night. At least the rest of us got a bit of sleep, after the doctor turned up.'

'I've taken the rest of the week off work,' said Mrs Bellingham. 'When the doctor popped back this afternoon, he said it wouldn't be wise to send her back to school till Monday and I reckon it'll be a struggle to get her there then.'

'Why? I thought . . .'

'Oh, she's fine, physically,' said Mrs Bellingham, sipping her coffee. 'But she's got it into her head that . . . that . . .'

'She thinks it was real, doesn't she? The night-mare?'

That much James had gleaned from a short conversation with Kits before he'd left for college.

'She's absolutely convinced. You wouldn't believe what she's had me doing today. I've had to buy every single newspaper. Listen to the radio news on the hour, every hour. Turn on the TV for the local reports. In the end, I even phoned the fire brigade to put her mind at rest. They must have thought I was mad. Excuse me, did you put out any fires last night? Only my daughter thought she saw one in a dream.'

'You didn't say that?'

'No. And they were very nice. But quite adamant. There were no fires. Not of any sort.'

'So what did Kits say to that?'

'Nothing, at first. But then she came up with a new theory. It was a future event, she'd seen. If the fire hadn't happened last night, it was going to happen. Sometime. And what's worse, she's decided it might have been her school she saw. You know . . . disabled people. Trapped.'

James sat for a moment, mulling it over.

'You don't think . . . I mean she's been right before and . . .'

'No, James, I don't!' said his mother. 'It was a nightmare. Nothing more. Nothing less. And you don't need to be a trained psychologist or dream

78

expert to know where it was coming from, do you? It's so obvious. Kits feels trapped by her disability. She's meeting more disabled people at that school than she knew existed before! That lad Paul, who talks to her on the bus. Two partially-sighted girls in her class. And, Kits was telling us, only the other day, about that kid who was left scarred and deaf from a firework explosion. It doesn't take a great leap of the imagination to turn that little lot into a nightmare about being trapped in a fire, now, does it? And Kits has never lacked imagination, has she?'

'No,' James conceded.

He had always considered imagination to be an asset. The sort of thing he didn't have. The sort of thing that helped you do well at school. But once that sensitivity was warped, traumatized . . . who knew what might happen?

'And then,' said his mother, 'in the middle of dealing with all that, the police phoned.'

'Oh?'

'Good news, in a way. Someone found an abandoned vehicle. Miles from here. Hidden. It was pretty burnt out but they traced it back to the owner who lives only a few streets away from Kits' old school. Forensic are still checking it but they don't hold out much hope.'

'And have they arrested him? Have they arrested the owner?'

'No. The car had been reported stolen two days

before the . . . accident. The owner couldn't have been driving it, at the time. Apart from anything else, he was still at work. Dozens of people saw him there.'

'So it doesn't really help?'

'It's better than nothing,' said Mrs Bellingham, unconvinced. 'I don't know why but I think if they could find the person who did it, it might help Kits to . . . come to terms with it better.'

'Lisa, too,' said James. 'Poor kid's completely screwed up, after what Kits said. She wants to come round but she's terrified of upsetting Kits again. And to cap it all, she's hung up on some guilt complex. I think she half believes Kits might have been right . . . about her holding something back.'

'That's crazy.'

'I know,' said James. 'When I think about it, when I think about the person responsible . . . I wish I could see him. Show him what he's done. To all of us. With his drink, drugs or sheer bloody carelessness. Then, other times, it's worse. Other times I think if I met him, I'd probably kill him.'

'James! Please . . .'

'I mean it, Mum. I mean it. When I think what Kits is going through, I know I could kill him.'

Mrs Bellingham shook her head, as James left the room. It wasn't only Kits who had changed. It was all of them. James, who lovingly carried spiders out of doors, rather than let her kill them. James who rescued birds off the cat and fought back tears when they died in his hands. The boy, who at six foot two and seventeen years of age, still cried at the end of sad films. Her son. Her son was talking about killing someone and meaning every word. What could she do?

The doctor had offered the services of a counsellor. Not just for Kits but for the whole family. She'd been against it, at first, insisting they had always been a close family. They would cope. Now she wasn't so sure.

By the weekend Mrs Bellingham was feeling a little more optimistic. After five days of scouring every line of every newspaper, Kits seemed to have given up. Accepted that it was an ordinary nightmare. Vivid. Terrifying. But a perfectly understandable result of her experiences. Not precognition. Not a prediction of the future.

Still, it had made them all uneasy. James and Lewis had crept around the house, barely daring to speak to Kits. Hating to watch her brood.

It was better now. James and Kits were in the lounge. Talking. Playing some hideous Grand Prix game on the computer. She had come to tell Kits that her friend Paul had phoned, asking why she hadn't been at school. She had reassured him that Kits was fine. That she'd be back on Monday.

Mrs Bellingham didn't go in immediately. She

paused in the doorway to watch. Listen. Grasping at any hint of a return to normality.

Two pairs of eyes were fixed on the computer screen. James was laughing.

'I don't believe I just did that!' he said. 'Your turn. Kits? Kits? Are you OK?'

'I saw them! I saw them again, on the screen. The eagle and the . . . James, did you see them? Did you?'

James looked at the racing cars. The same cars that had been there all the time. Cars not eagles.

'Er no, what do you . . . ?'

'James,' she said urgently. 'I've got to see Lisa. I've got to see her now.'

'Hey,' said James, trying to force his brain to catch up with this latest outburst. 'Slow down. What do you mean? Eagles? Lisa?'

Kits put her head in her hands. She'd done it again. Blurted something out, before stopping to think. And now she'd have to try to explain. But how much should she say?

They thought she was mad enough, as it was. After the fire business. And she hadn't told them the half of it. Only about what she'd seen. Not how she'd seen it. She couldn't bring herself to mention the floating. And now? If she told James what she'd been seeing. What she'd just seen again. The same thing she'd been seeing for two days now.

Kits uncovered her face. Stared at James. Tried to speak calmly.

'Lisa's in danger. I've got to see her. I've got to warn her.'

Mrs Bellingham's blood seemed to freeze as she listened. Should she go in? Put a stop to it? She waited for James's response.

'Danger?' said James. 'What sort of danger?'

'I don't know exactly. I keep seeing these pictures. In my head, on the bedroom wall, on the screen. And every time I see them, I hear Lisa screaming out. She's terrified . . . she . . .'

At that moment James looked towards the door. Caught his mother's eye. Saw the pain cross her face.

'No,' said James. 'Please, Kits. You know that's not possible.'

'It's possible because it happens. It started last night. I woke up. I saw this enormous bird, painted on the bedroom wall. An eagle with its wings stretched out. I thought I was dreaming . . .'

'That's it,' said James. 'It was a dream. Another dream.'

'And then, Lisa called out to me. Telling me to get it away from her. It was attacking her.'

'That sort of proves it then, doesn't it,' said James, trying to lighten the tone. 'I mean we don't exactly get a lot of eagles round here, do we? And they very rarely attack people. It was a dream.'

'That's what I told myself. Then this morning, the pictures came back, in my head. An eagle and a . . .'

'They came back because you were brooding about the dream.'

'But they kept coming back. All day. And then a minute ago, I saw them as clear as day on the screen. And Lisa was screaming . . .'

It was too much for for Mrs Bellingham. She had to intervene.

'Oh, Kits,' she said, rushing in, kneeling beside her chair. 'Don't you see, love? You've been fretting about Lisa ever since that last visit. She screamed when you insisted she was lying, remember? It's all got mixed up in your head, that's all. Lisa's not in any danger. Nothing's going to happen.'

'And what about the eagle? Where's that coming from?'

'I don't know. But James is right. Lisa's hardly going to come across one, is she?'

'She could do,' said Kits, sullenly. 'What if she went to a zoo . . . a bird sanctuary. Anyway the eagle might not be real. It might just be a symbol. And there was something else . . .'

'Symbol,' her mother interrupted. 'That's more like it. Don't you see, love? They're all symbols. All the things you see. It's just your own fears and frustrations getting the better of you. Have one of your tab . . .'

'I don't need tablets!'

'All right . . . don't get worked up, again.'

'I shouldn't have said anything. I shouldn't have told you. I knew what you'd say. I knew you wouldn't believe me.'

'It's not that we don't believe you,' said James. 'But, think about it, Kits. Mum's right. What you see, what you hear . . . they're not necessarily predictions. Think how vivid that fire was to you and nothing's happened, has it?'

'Not yet.'

'It's not going to. And nothing's going to happen to Lisa.'

'Are you sure?' said Kits, staring at him.

'No,' said James. 'Nobody can ever be sure of anything, can they? But I should think it's a fairly safe bet. She'll probably phone tonight or tomorrow and when she does I'll make sure everything's OK.'

'And what if she doesn't phone? I've no way of getting in touch. You know Lisa. She won't give her phone number to anyone. Her mother won't let her. They're ex-directory. How will I know she's all right?'

'Listen,' said James. 'If she hasn't phoned in a day or two I'll phone the school. And if she's not at school I'll go round to her house.'

'Why not now?' said Kits. 'Why can't we go now?'

'No,' said Mrs Bellingham firmly. 'You've got to get a grip, love. You've got to face up to these – these dreams – for what they are. Your own fears and frustrations coming to the surface. There are no fires. No eagles. And Lisa isn't in any danger. Do you understand?'

'I'm trying to,' said Kits, starting to cry. 'But nothing makes sense any more.'

CHAPTER EIGHT

James looked at the number of the house. 43. Lisa lived at 49. He didn't move immediately. He felt sure he wouldn't be welcome. He barely knew what to say. But, after what had happened, he had to come.

Kits had settled down on Sunday night after Lisa had phoned, apparently in good spirits and with no obvious problems. In fact Kits had been so settled that she'd slept through the night, the first full night without waking, since the accident. On Monday she'd gone back to school. It had gone better than expected.

On Tuesday she'd come back chattering about chess club and how Paul had stepped up his campaign to interest her in swimming. She was obviously talking to people more. Had actually given Paul's suggestion some consideration. OK, so she'd eventually decided against it, but there was hope.

Then the bombshell had hit. This morning, James had woken to his radio alarm as usual.

Listened to the music as he got dressed. Robbie Williams. He even remembered who it was. Funny. He'd have thought that what happened next would have eclipsed Robbie Williams from his mind. The news. The local news. News of a fire in an old people's home, a couple of miles from where they lived. A fire which had happened during the night. Exactly a week since Kits' dream.

He'd rushed round the house, alerting his parents and Lewis to turn off all the radios. Not to let Kits hear. It was coincidence, of course. A bizarre, stupid, tragic, crazy coincidence. But he'd left the house in a daze. Headed straight for the common room at college. Caught the news again, in full. The fire brigade had been on the scene in minutes. Mercifully they'd got everyone out safely in the end but it had been touch and go. Two elderly residents had been trapped . . .

Trapped. They were all trapped now. Trapped in whatever crazy thing had happened to Kits. Trapped into believing. Not believing.

Kits believed. They'd been stupid to try to keep it from her. Paul, not knowing about the dream, had mentioned it, in the mini-bus on the way to school. Kits had gone hysterical. The driver had got her to the school but she'd had to be brought straight home.

Their mother had tried to convince her it was another coincidence, explaining what she firmly believed herself. That, if you looked long enough, you'd find something to fit every dream, every nightmare you ever had. There was nothing to link Kits' nightmare with . . .

'They were disabled. In a big house. More or less where I said it was,' Kits had screamed at that point. 'What more evidence do you want?'

She'd taken one of the sedatives, which she increasingly needed, but had remained restless for a while.

'You believe me, don't you, James? Oh, don't look at her. Don't look at Mum. I want to know what you think.'

He hadn't known what to think. What to say. The build-up of coincidence was beginning to defy even his, normally unimaginative, mind. But the alternative? That Kits was, in some way, psychic. That she could see the future. No way! It wasn't possible.

Then why was he here? Standing outside Lisa's house. Coming to check that everything was OK. All because the coincidence of the fire had refuelled Kits' belief that Lisa was in trouble. That the eagle had been yet another premonition.

But was it only because Kits had insisted? Was he really starting to get sucked in? Did he really expect to find Lisa in some sort of danger? Grappling with an escaped eagle, perhaps? Or maybe he just wanted to see her anyway. For some crazy reason of his own, he'd missed having Lisa around.

He walked up the path towards the small terraced house and rang the doorbell. Lisa opened the door immediately. No. Not Lisa. It took him a couple of seconds to register his mistake. Same dark hair, though cut shorter than Lisa's. Enormous brown eyes. Slim figure. Clearly older than Lisa. Did Lisa have a sister? She'd never mentioned a sister. But then Lisa had said so little about her family.

'Yes,' the person at the door said eyeing him with obvious suspicion.

'Er . . . is Lisa in?'

'Yes.'

'I'm James. James Bellingham. Katherine's brother.'

Still no invitation to go inside.

'Is Lisa busy? Can I have a word with her?'

'Lisa! Someone to see you.'

There was only room in the doorway for one person. The lookalike stepped back as Lisa appeared.

'What are you doing here?' Lisa hissed.

'Can I come in? I'm freezing.'

'I don't know. Mum doesn't like . . .'

'That was your mother?' James whispered, sensing that she was still lurking close by. 'She only looks about twenty-five!'

'You're not far wrong. She's thirty-one.'

90

James was doing a quick calculation. She must only have been sixteen, seventeen, when Lisa was born.

'Look,' said Lisa, glancing round, nervously. 'You can come in, for a minute.'

She ushered him into the lounge, where two small boys were playing. Almost immediately her mother called her and she disappeared, slamming the door behind her.

James heard raised voices. Two. Shrill. Female.

He couldn't catch what they were saying, so focused his attention on the little boys. Twins, Kits had once told him. Identical twins by the look of it. Dressed alike in Thomas the Tank Engine pyjamas. Gingery, curly hair. They were playing with some Duplo. Or rather one of them was.

As he watched, it wasn't difficult to spot that the twins behaved quite differently. One was busy, fitting wheels onto bricks. Taking them off again. Trying something else. The other sat there, placidly watching. Barely watching, in fact. His hazel eyes were dull and vacant. He was sitting incredibly still. Not like a child at all.

'Want to play?' said the active one.

It took James a moment to realize that the invitation was to him, not to the passive brother.

'OK,' he said.

There wasn't much else to do with Lisa and her mother still shrieking somewhere out the back.

'What are you making?'

'It's a spaceship, see?' said the boy in clear, though child-like speech. 'That's the engine. An' it's got wings. But I don't know whether it should have wheels.'

'Would it need wheels in space?'

'No, silly,' said the boy. 'But it might when it lands.'

'We'd better have them, then,' said James, smiling. 'What's your name?'

'Liam.'

'And what's your name?' said James to the quieter one.

'That's Toby.'

'Would you like to make something, Toby?' James asked.

The boy looked at him. He had clearly heard but seemed not to understand the question.

'He doesn't talk,' said Liam.

'Doesn't talk?' said James. 'Not ever?'

'Nope.'

'Why?'

'Don't know,' said Liam, as if it didn't much matter. 'Shall we put some lights on?'

'Lights,' said James, barely concentrating. 'Yes. I suppose a spaceship should have lights.'

He was building with Liam but his thoughts were on Toby. When Kits had told him about Lisa's brothers, she hadn't mentioned anything special,

92

had she? Like one of them didn't speak. Did Kits know? Perhaps Lisa hadn't confided in her. Or maybe Liam was making it up. Maybe Toby was just shy, like Lisa. Yet, looking at him, he knew it was more than that. Toby was completely engulfed in some private world of his own.

James had heard of cases of twins behaving strangely. Some developed forms of private communication. Often one was dominant and the other passive. But this looked like an extreme case. He wondered whether Toby's problem was psychological or physical.

He stretched out his hand and offered Toby some bricks. The boy screamed, leapt up and ran from the room.

Liam barely noticed.

'Blast off!' he shouted, waving the spaceship above his head. 'Let's make another.'

There was no time for more spaceships. Lisa's mother came in, snatched Liam up in her arms, as if James were some sort of child molester, and darted from the room without a word.

James was staring after her, open-mouthed, when Lisa returned and sank into a chair.

'Thanks a lot,' she snarled.

'Why . . . what . . . ?'

'You must have heard!'

'I heard shouting, that's all. What's wrong? What's happened?'

'You happened, that's what. You came round. And I had to explain you.'

'Explain me?'

'I never even told her Kits had a brother. Not an older one. I mentioned Lewis, I think, but not you. Now Mum thinks you're a boyfriend I've been hiding away.'

'Hiding away? Lisa, you're fifteen. Even if I was your boyfriend surely she couldn't stop you . . .'

'She couldn't actually stop me, no. But if you knew the trouble the mere mention of a male name causes. I can't even talk about the lanky, spotty lads in my class without her accusing me of carrying on with them. You wouldn't believe the names she calls me. She's a headcase, James, honestly. I'm not gonna stick it much longer, I tell you. I'm gonna run away. Have myself put into care or something.'

James was silent for a moment. Did Lisa mean it? Was this what Kits was on about? Was this the trouble she reckoned she sensed? And what the heck did it have to do with eagles?

'Are you serious?'

'Dead right I am.'

'It can't be that bad.'

'Can't it? What the hell do you know about it?'

'Nothing. Because you don't ever let anyone that close, do you? Not even Kits.'

The mention of Kits brought an immediate change in Lisa, her anger giving way to anxiety.

'How is she? There's nothing wrong is there? I can't believe I've been so selfish droning on about my problems . . . you've come to tell me something about Kits, haven't you?'

'Yes,' said James. 'But don't panic. Nothing's wrong as such. Listen, I know it's awkward but you couldn't come back with me for an hour, could you? I think it would help Kits if she could see you. You know what she's like these days. She gets worked up about things. At the moment, she's worrying about you.'

He didn't go into any details about dreams and eagles. He didn't have to. Lisa answered almost immediately.

'Yeah, OK. Why not?'

'What about your mum? What will you tell her?'

'I won't tell her anything. If I tried there'd be a row. She's putting the boys to bed. I'll scribble a quick note. There'll be hell on when I get back. If I come back. But who cares? Come on. Quick before she gets down.'

James felt faintly embarrassed absconding from the house, knowing that Lisa's mum objected. On the other hand, it was clearly ridiculous. You couldn't keep a fifteen-year-old girl locked up. And she was as safe with him as she'd be with anyone.

James guided Lisa to where he'd parked the car. He drove quite slowly, carefully. It wasn't long since he'd passed his test, and, truth be known, he'd become nervous of driving, since what had happened to Kits.

They kept the conversation light, talking about ordinary, everyday things. Lisa asked about college. Told him school was a bit grim since Kits had gone. Told him she'd persevered with netball, gymnastics, all the things she and Kits used to do together. It was hard, but in a funny way, she felt it kept her in touch somehow.

Kits was in her room when they got back. James showed Lisa in, grabbed some drinks and biscuits, came back and sat down. He hadn't been invited but neither of the girls seemed to object, so he stayed.

'How've you been?' Lisa was asking Kits, quietly, awkwardly.

'Not brilliant,' said Kits. 'OK, physically. The doctors reckon I'm making a bit of progress but I keep having these sort of dream things . . . did James tell you?'

'I didn't really have time,' James said. 'There was a bit of hassle with . . .'

He looked at Lisa, wondering whether he ought to go on.

'It's all right,' said Lisa. 'I guess I owe you some sort of explanation.'

Before James could protest that Lisa didn't need to explain anything if she didn't want to, she was outlining what had happened to Kits.

'The thing is,' Lisa ended. 'It was my fault. I shouldn't have left James alone with the twins. Poor Toby's really nervous. Especially with blokes.'

'Why?' said Kits.

'It's a long story,' said Lisa. 'And not a very pleasant one either. It's not something I normally talk about. But I've been practising. The psychologist dragged it all out of me. Said it would help. That it was all tied up together. My anger with Mum, my guilt feelings about the accident and about Toby . . . Look, I'm sorry. I came here to cheer you up not to drivel on about my problems.'

Kits stared at Lisa, forcing herself to think before she spoke. She didn't want to scare Lisa off. She could feel her already withdrawing. Trying to push back the tidal waves of pain and hurt which were threatening to engulf them both.

'No, please,' she said quietly. 'I'd like to know. I'd like you to tell me.'

CHAPTER NINE

'I don't quite know where to start,' said Lisa, looking first at Kits and then at James. 'I suppose the beginning's not a bad place . . . but it's not like a made-up story, is it? It's hard to know when the beginning was. Probably before I was even born. You gathered Mum was pretty young when she had me.'

James nodded.

'So, when I was little, I had a mum and a dad. We lived in Sheffield. I was an ordinary kid, going to an ordinary school, doing ordinary things. Thinking I was happy in my own shy, quiet way. I don't remember any rows, any hassle. Nothing mega, anyway. In fact, I don't remember much about those early days. Funny, isn't it? Eight years pass in a rosy haze of thinking everything's well with your little world, then suddenly, bang! Something happens that changes everything.'

'Like the accident,' said Kits quietly.

'Yeah,' said Lisa. 'That's what the psychologist said. She said I might have blocked the accident out because of that. Because my mind's already too full of other bad memories. I couldn't cope with any more. She reckons I need to talk more. Get it all out in the open . . .'

James and Kits sat, waiting for Lisa to carry on.

'It was a Tuesday. A week after my eighth birthday. I remember racing out of school, clutching a painting, staring around for Mum, desperate to show her. It was a castle I'd painted. With knights on horseback and everything. My teacher had held it up for everyone to see. Said I had real talent.'

Kits nodded. She'd seen Lisa's artwork. She really did have talent.

'Anyway, Mum wasn't there. I couldn't under-stand it. I don't think there'd ever been a time when she wasn't there to meet me. I panicked. Started crying. Then Mrs Chase, who lived down the bottom of our road, came over and grabbed my hand. Said I was to go home with her. Not to worry but that Mum wasn't too well. She put my hand on the handles of a double buggy she was pushing. She had five kids of her own. Two in the pushchair and three lads she'd just picked up from school. I dropped my painting,' said Lisa, as tears started to form in her eyes. 'I dropped my painting and we just left it there, in the road, with cars running over it.'

Kits didn't know what to say. Lisa's words were

sad enough but it was worse than that. She was picking up all the feelings. She was eight again, with Lisa, confused and frightened.

'Mrs Chase took me home with her. It was good of her, I suppose, with five rowdy kids of her own but, for me, it was like walking into some sort of hell. Everyone screaming and fighting – the over-powering stench of baby puke and dirty nappies . . . And she gave us all cold baked beans, straight out of the tin for tea.'

Lisa laughed and wiped her eyes with her hand.

'Maybe my therapist was right,' she said. 'Maybe it does help to talk about it. I've never been able to laugh about the Chases' house before. I mean these things seem pretty serious when you're only eight and as far as you know both parents have disap-peared off the ends of the earth. I kept expecting Dad to turn up but he didn't. Eventually Mr Chase came in from work and started bathing the kids. Then Mrs Chase sits me down and tells me Mum's in hospital. Nothing serious, she said. She'll be out in a day or two.'

Kits had a million questions she wanted to ask but she resisted the temptation to try to hurry Lisa's story.

'I stayed there for three days,' said Lisa. 'All the time asking to see Mum, asking where my dad was. Not believing when Mrs Chase hugged me and said it would all be all right.'

Lisa paused, sipped her drink, coughed.

'No-one told me what was wrong with my mum. Not even Mum when she came out and took me home. I didn't find out until years afterwards, though by then, of course, I'd started to guess. Mum had taken an overdose – tried to kill herself.'

'Kill herself?' Kits breathed. 'Why?'

'Dad had upped and left,' said Lisa. 'Not that she even told me that, for ages. Said he'd had to go away for a while. Told me all sorts of lies for months . . .'

'Maybe she was trying to protect you!' said Kits.

'Maybe,' said Lisa, now totally involved in the past. 'But it didn't feel that way. And when she finally told me that he'd left us to live with someone else, I didn't believe her. I wanted to see him. I knew he'd want to see me. I thought she wouldn't let him. That she was keeping me away from him. That's when things really started to go wrong with me and Mum. I was screaming, crying all the time, demanding to see him until finally she'd had enough and she told me the truth.'

'"Give it a break, Lisa," she screamed at me one day. "I don't know why you think he's so flaming wonderful. He's not even your real dad."'

Kits felt as though a knife had plunged into her as Lisa spoke.

'I don't think she meant to tell me,' said Lisa. 'But once she had, she tried to explain it all. My real dad apparently was someone she'd been going out with at school. They were about your age, James, just starting A-levels, when she realized she was pregnant.

'Mum left school, had a massive row with her family, walked out and hasn't seen them since. He, of course, was fine. Did his exams and buzzed off to university. They lost touch and that was that. About a year after I was born, Mum started living with Dean. The one I thought was my dad. Are you following all this?'

Kits nodded.

'So Dean didn't think he had any responsibility for me, see? He'd never officially adopted me or anything. I used his name. Mountjoy. I still do. But he's not my real dad. Never was. Him and Mum weren't even married. Not that I believed a word of it, when Mum first told me. I thought it was all an elaborate lie to stop me wanting to see him.'

'And are you sure . . . ?' Kits began.

She stopped. She had been about to ask whether Lisa was sure it was true. It seemed, to Kits, impossible for a bloke to abandon completely a kid he'd brought up as his own for seven years. It seemed far more likely that Lisa's mum had refused him access. But even as she started to speak, she felt an emptiness of loss, screaming out from every pore in Lisa's body and knew it was true.

'I'm sure now,' said Lisa, 'because of what happened later. But at the time, I hated her.

Especially when she took up with Ross, a few months later. Before I knew what was happening, he'd moved in with us. Next thing I know, she's pregnant with the twins and she's getting married. I don't know who I hated most. Her or Ross. He was . . . he . . .'

Lisa fell silent. Kits and James waited, glancing at each other, both fearful of what might be coming next.

'At first,' Lisa said, 'it was just a feeling. I don't think I had any real reason to hate him except that Mum was so wrapped up in him. He'd taken Dean's place. So I guess I just got hung up on all the usual things kids get hung up about in the merry-go-round of grown-up relationships.

'But then I started to notice things Mum didn't seem to see or care about. Ross drank a lot. His language was foul. He was forever borrowing money off her or just taking it out of her purse. I didn't know what Mum saw in him. He was good looking, I suppose, in a rough sort of way. But I reckon it was a real rebound thing. First person who came along after she'd been let down, again.

'Anyway, I went off the rails a bit. I was playing up something chronic. Pestering to see my dad . . . well, Dean. I wasn't easy to live with . . .'

'I'm not surprised!' said James.

'So then, Ross started hitting me.'

Kits shuddered. Violence was alien to her.

Nobody had ever hit her or James or Lewis.

'What did your mum . . . ?'

'She didn't know,' said Lisa, defensively. 'At least, I don't think so. Not at first. He never did it when she was around.'

'Didn't you tell her?'

'Not straight away. I knew she wouldn't believe me. That she'd say I deserved it, or something. I hated them both so much. I didn't even let on when my teacher spotted the bruises. She got my mum in and started asking questions. I said I'd fallen over, banged into things. All sorts of rubbish.'

'Why?'

'I was scared, I suppose. Not so much of Ross. I could put up with the thumping and kicking, or so I thought. I was scared of my mum. I was scared she'd send me away.'

'But surely she wouldn't have done that,' said Kits.

'I know it sounds crazy,' Lisa protested. 'But I was only little, remember. Younger than your Lewis is now. You don't really think things out. My behaviour had got worse. Mum used to scream at me. Say awful things. About putting me into care and stuff. I don't think she'd have actually done it. But I did at the time.'

'I don't believe I'm hearing this,' said James, getting up and pacing round the room. 'I can't believe . . . no wonder you don't get on. Why didn't you tell us . . . why didn't you tell Kits?'

'No point,' said Lisa shrugging. 'There's nothing anyone can do. Not now. And besides, it's not the sort of thing you want to dredge up all the time. Once it's over, you just push it to the back of your mind – well, as far as it will go – and try to get on with life. I wanted to forget. I wouldn't be talking about it now if the psychologist hadn't started asking all those questions. Once it's back in your mind, it sort of takes over.'

'So how long did all this go on for?' said James, flopping into his chair again. 'All this abuse?'

'Ross calmed down, for a bit, after the twins were born,' said Lisa. 'I think we all did. I'd been working myself up to hate the babies but I found that I couldn't. They gave me a sort of outlet. Something to do. Someone to play with. They came at the right time. I'd outgrown dolls and here was the real thing. I was hooked. I did all sorts for them. And that gave Mum and Ross more time to themselves, so everybody was happy. I still didn't like Ross. I didn't like the way he looked at me. He'd walk into the bathroom when I was showering . . .'

'He didn't . . . you're not saying . . .' Kits began tuning into Lisa's emotions trying to sense just how bad it had been.

'No. He never actually touched me. Not like that. I think he might have done. Given time. I don't know. I kept away from him as much as I could but then it got more difficult. He lost his job. Mum took on extra work in the evenings. Ross was supposed to look after us.'

Lisa stopped again, staring into space, struggling with the memories. Wanting to let them out. Wanting to keep them in.

'Half the time he didn't. He went out. Left us on our own. I didn't mind. I preferred it that way. I could look after the twins, no problem. It wasn't so easy when he was there. He didn't like them crying. Wouldn't change them or feed them. Got mad if I wasn't quick enough, if one was left crying while I saw to the other. It's tricky with two.'

'Tricky!' said James his head almost exploding at the sheer idea of leaving a child to cope with two babies.

'James!' said Kits irritated by the interruption. 'Just let Lisa tell us, will you?'

'One night,' said Lisa, 'Liam started crying. I took him to the bathroom to see if he needed changing and then Toby started off. I was busy with Liam, so I couldn't get there straight away. When I did he was there. Ross. He had Toby. He was shaking him over and over. I screamed at him to stop. He froze. Dumped Toby in his cot, pushed past me and went out.'

'Is that why . . . is that . . . ?' James began.

He stopped as Kits glared at him. Lisa had gone white. Her hand was shaking.

106

'Toby was OK,' said Lisa. 'I put them both in the pram and went to the supermarket where Mum worked. I told her. I told her what he'd done and she didn't believe me. She called me a liar over and over on the way home. And then, the next night, he started on me again. She'd told him! She'd told him what I'd said.'

'Couldn't you . . . ?' James clenched his fists, digging his nails into his palms. He was trying to stay quiet, trying not to interrupt but it was so difficult. So impossible.

'Don't say it,' Lisa snapped. 'Don't say it, James. I know now what I should have done. I should have gone to my teacher. To the police. The doctor. Someone. Anyone. But I didn't. I didn't go to anyone at first, until I saw him hit Liam. By then I was desperate. I went rooting around in my mum's stuff until I found my dad's, Dean's, phone number, I phoned him up. I tried to tell him. I said I needed him . . .'

She barely needed to go on. You didn't have to be particularly psychic to know what had happened. Kits knew, James knew, without Lisa saying it. They knew what Dean had done.

'That's when I knew that Mum hadn't lied to me,' Lisa said, her voice dropping to a whisper. 'He wasn't my dad. Didn't want to be. All those years he'd spent with us. All those years I thought he loved me, were the lie. Do you want to know what he said to me? Do you want to know what he said before he put the phone down?'

Kits didn't think she did. To imagine was bad enough. But Lisa went on.

'"Tell your mum," he said, "you're nothing to do with me, Lisa. Tell your mum and don't phone me again."'

James moved from his seat putting his arm around Lisa as she started to cry.

'I'm sorry,' she said.

'Don't be,' said James. 'You don't need to apologize. I just wish you'd told us . . . told Kits before. But I suppose it's hard to trust anyone after that.'

'It's not that,' said Lisa, 'I do trust you. Both of you. I know I can't hate everyone in the world because of Dean and Ross and the dad who didn't even stick around long enough to meet me. But Mum doesn't see it like that. She's given up on people. Men especially. And she wants me to be the same. She goes hysterical at the mere mention of a boyfriend. Throws a fit if I wear make-up. Calls my clothes tarty. Questions every move I make. And the worst thing is, I actually understand it. I can't put up with it. I can't live my life that way. But I know what she's doing.'

Lisa paused.

'It's not just with me, either. She's as bad with the boys. They don't play out. Don't go anywhere with anyone. They go to school and that's it. She takes them and she brings them back. She's given up work. She's with them all the time. She's stifling them, like she tries to stifle me. Because she feels guilty. She's trying to make up for not being there when we needed her. But she'll never make it up. Not to Toby anyway. You've seen how he is, James.'

'I've seen it,' said James. 'But I'm not sure . . .'

'Brain damage,' said Lisa. 'He's never going to get any better. Ross was bound to go too far with one of us. I tried to tell her. Over and over I tried. Ross was getting worse. Hitting me. Slapping the twins. That's what I couldn't stand. When he hit them. They were babies, barely six months old. I did all sorts. Tried to hide them. Took them out for walks at night. Even the neighbours were getting suspicious. But Mum didn't see. Didn't want to see.'

Kits shuffled in her chair. It was all getting too intense. She wasn't only hearing, as James was, she was picking up all the feelings, all the pain that was threatening to tear her apart. And if it was like this for her, sensing it second-hand, what on earth must it be like for Lisa, reliving every dreadful minute?

'It was a neighbour who came round that night,' Lisa was saying. 'Ross had come in drunk. It was still early, though, I think. The twins were asleep. I thought they'd be OK. But he woke them up. Drooling and slavering over them. Of course, they started to cry. I got Liam out of the way but it was too late. He'd picked Toby up. Shook him. Threw him across the room. Picked him up again. Started shaking him. I was screaming. Biting. Kicking. Anything to make him stop.'

Lisa started to cry again. James sat with her, holding her hand.

'You don't have to go on,' said Kits, as much to protect herself as Lisa.

'No. I want to,' said Lisa. 'It's helping, honest. I need to tell you the whole story, now. It's almost over. Our neighbour, Mr Fairly, came rushing in. He had a key. For emergencies – though I don't suppose they ever expected . . . His wife had phoned the police . . . Mr Fairly grabbed Toby . . . we got him to hospital . . . the police picked Ross up later . . . he'd rushed out . . . it's all confused . . . I . . .'

'OK,' said James. 'Slowly. Take it slowly.'

'Toby almost died. I sometimes think it would have been better if . . . No. That's not true. We love Toby. But what sort of a life is he ever going to have? What's going to happen when he gets older?'

She paused again, for a moment, lost in thought.

'He denied it, of course. Ross denied it. But he couldn't get away with it. There was my evidence. And Mr Fairly's. I had to go to court. I never saw Ross there. They keep you separate. I don't remember all the details but he got a pretty light sentence – considering. His lawyer spun this sob story about Ross's tragic background. How he'd been battered himself, as a child. How he'd been put in care as a teenager. How it was his first serious offence . . . how sorry he was. Sorry!'

Lisa paused for a moment, pulling a tissue out of her bag. Wiping her eyes.

'Ross wasn't sorry! He wrote to Mum, once, from prison. Blaming it all on me. She'd seen the light, then, though. When it was too late. Got a court order banning him from writing or coming near us ever again. Mum's never quite sure though. Never feels settled or easy. Even though he's still inside. That's why we move around so much.'

'I can't believe it,' said Kits quietly. 'I can't believe you've been through all this and never said . . .'

'Like I told you. It's best not to dwell on it. I wouldn't be telling you now if it hadn't been for the accident, if that psychologist hadn't dragged it all up. Reckons I'm hooked on guilt, see? She says I blame myself for my birth dad and Dean going away. For spoiling my mum's relationship with Ross. For not doing enough to stop him battering the twins. For getting him put away. For hating my mum still.'

'But none of it's your fault,' Kits insisted. 'Surely you must see that?'

'That's what she says. The head doctor. But she

111

reckons I'm still all wound up in it. That's why I feel guilty about the accident. That's why I've blocked the memories. In case it turns out that I'm in some way responsible for that too.'

'But you can't be,' said Kits. 'You might have seen something, you might know something, you might even be holding something back – but none of that makes you responsible. Don't you see, Lisa? It all makes sense now.'

'Does it?'

'Of course it does . . . I wish I'd known . . . I wish I'd bothered to think . . . I wish I'd understood all this before . . . You're blocking out the accident because you can't face any more pain. It's nothing sinister. You're not hiding anything. And there's no way, no way on earth that you were responsible. It's not possible.'

'It doesn't have to be possible, Kits,' said Lisa, quietly. 'It doesn't have to be rational. We're not talking cosy, happy family sort of rationality here. We're talking seriously unbalanced nutters.'

CHAPTER TEN

'I have to go,' said Lisa, looking at her watch. 'It's late. Mum'll be frantic.'

'I'll drive you,' said James.

'Thanks,' said Lisa. 'But just to the end of my road. I don't want Mum seeing you again.'

'OK,' said James. 'But you'll be all right, won't you? With your mum? You're not going to . . .'

'I'm not going to run away, if that's what you mean,' said Lisa, smiling. 'Not tonight. I'm too tired!'

'Run away?' said Kits, anxiously. 'Surely . . .'

'No,' said Lisa, not wanting to upset Kits with yet more of her problems. 'It was just some stupid thing I said to James earlier.'

'And Lisa,' Kits added, as they were about to leave.

'Yes?'

'Have you got any school trips coming up or anything?'

'No, I don't think so, why?'

'You're not planning to go anywhere near a zoo or a bird sanctuary, are you?'

'Er . . . no,' said Lisa, looking at James, to explain this latest weird outburst from Kits.

'Never mind,' said James, grabbing Lisa's arm and steering her out. 'Just promise me you'll phone if there are any problems, OK?'

James seemed to be away for ages. Kits watched the news, to try to take her mind off things. She talked to Lewis for a bit when he came in to say goodnight, did some homework and finally shouted to Mum to help her get ready for bed. A slow business, these days, but she was still washed, changed and in bed, by the time James came back. They spoke, only briefly. James, as always, had college work to catch up on. So Kits lay awake into the early hours, brooding about Lisa.

She'd been right. Lisa was in trouble. But not the sort of immediate danger her dreams had led her to believe. Lisa's screams were coming from the past not the future but it didn't make them less real. How did Lisa cope?

Maybe you learnt to cope with mental scars, just the way she was learning to cope with her physical disability. She could do all sorts of things for herself now. Put most of her clothes on, unaided . . . manage in the newly-adapted bathroom . . . make herself drinks and snacks. These optimistic thoughts finally lulled Kits into sleep. She was learning to cope. It was slow, it was frustrating, but she was learning, just as Lisa was learning.

Her thoughts were still on Lisa, when she woke. She'd had the dream again. Seen the images, heard the screams. It disturbed her but she managed to go about her morning routine calmly. It wasn't too bad when you knew where the nightmares were coming from. Lisa was OK, in the short term, though the long term just didn't bear thinking about.

Kits surprised her mother by doing more for herself than usual. She even seemed keen to go to school, propelling her wheelchair to the door as the bell rang. But it wasn't the driver of her mini-bus who was waiting. It was two police officers.

Kits let them in and followed them to the kitchen. This could be news about the stolen car. Not good news. You didn't have to be especially psychic to know that the police officers looked anxious rather than elated. Still, their first words surprised her.

'It's about Lisa Mountjoy,' the lady said.

'Lisa?' Kits repeated, as the whole family gathered round.

'She didn't go home last night.'

'Oh, no!' said James.

'James,' said Kits. 'I thought you dropped her off. You said . . .'

'I did drop her off,' said James. 'At the end of her

street, like we agreed. I even watched her go in the gate before I drove off!'

'Hold on, slow down a minute,' said the policeman. 'Lisa's mother said you turned up at their house about seven o'clock and that she went off with you.'

'We came here,' said James. 'Kits wanted to see Lisa. I drove her here.'

'Then what?'

'We talked for a while . . . an hour or so, that's all. Then I drove her home.'

'And what time was that?'

'Not late. She'd had a row with her mum. Didn't want to be late. Didn't want to make it worse. It was about . . .'

'Nine,' said Kits. 'I watched the nine o'clock news just after they left.'

'And what time did you get back, after dropping Lisa off?' the policeman asked James.

'I don't know,' James said, looking at Kits. 'Ten, maybe later. Maybe more like half past.'

'It took you an hour and a half to drive her home and get back?' said the policeman. 'Yet it's only a fifteen-minute drive.'

'We talked for a while, when I stopped the car,' said James. 'She'd been telling us a whole load of things about her past – she was upset. We talked. Then I stopped for petrol on the way back. Mum had given me money to fill the tank. I ended up

116

having a cup of coffee with the guy at the garage. He's a mate of mine. From college. Does shifts at the garage at night.'

'And he'll confirm this, I suppose,' said the police officer.

'Of course he'll confirm it,' said James. 'What the hell are you suggesting?'

'I'm not suggesting anything, yet,' the officer replied. 'Now you say Lisa had a row at home? Before she came here?'

'She's always having rows at home,' said Kits. 'She doesn't get on with her mum.'

'Right,' said the policeman. 'I need to know all the details. Everything Lisa did or said, last night.'

James nodded. The doorbell rang again. Mrs Bellingham answered it.

'Katherine won't be coming to school today,' she told the mini-bus driver. 'I'll phone in later to explain.'

Only Lewis went out early that morning. The rest of them stayed at home waiting for the doorbell or the phone to ring.

'I was right,' Kits cried. 'The dream, the pictures . . . I should have known . . . I should have done something . . .'

'Listen,' said Mrs Bellingham, putting her hands, firmly, on Kits' shoulders. 'I know you're worried. I know you're upset but this sort of hysteria won't

117

help. I'm going to go round and see Lisa's mum, OK? From what you said, she doesn't have much by way of family and friends. She might appreciate some support.'

Mrs Bellingham returned much more quickly than Kits had expected, deflated and depressed. Her offers of help, reassurance had been rejected. Lisa's mum hadn't even let her in the house. She'd stood in the doorway screaming abuse, mainly levelled at James. She'd accused James of having some sort of relationship with Lisa. Had virtually accused the family of having Lisa with them. Or, at least of knowing where she was.

By midday, they were all frantic. James was convinced Lisa had run away. He persuaded his dad to go down town with him. Search the coffee bars. The precinct. Anywhere that Lisa might be.

In the afternoon, the police returned.

'We've spoken to Lisa's mother again,' they said. 'It seems she thinks you and Lisa had some sort of relationship going on behind her back.'

'I got that too,' Mrs Bellingham said. 'But it simply isn't true. Lisa is my daughter's friend. She used to spend a lot of time here. Treated it as a second home until recently. She hasn't been coming so often since Kits' accident. I'm afraid nobody's been quite themselves. Poor Lisa apparently felt terribly guilty – though she'd no reason to, of course.'

'Of course,' the policeman repeated.

He was familiar with the details of Katherine Bellingham's accident. There was no reason to think the two incidents were related. But you could never be sure.

'But Lisa came here, again, last night,' he said.

'Like we told you,' said James.

'What you didn't tell me was that you and Lisa quarrelled last night, when you took her home.'

'James?' said Kits, questioning him with her eyes.

'We didn't!' James insisted. 'Why should I quarrel with Lisa?'

'An elderly lady out walking her dog said she saw you and Lisa about ten o'clock, in the street behind Lisa's. She said you grabbed hold of her arm. That she got back in the car.'

'Rubbish,' said James. 'I don't know who or what she thought she saw but it wasn't me and Lisa! I never even left the car! Lisa got out and walked off. I waved. That was it. And by ten o'clock I was in the garage talking to Dave.'

'He confirms that you were there but says he can't be sure of the time.'

'I'm not sure!' said James. 'You don't look at your watch every flaming minute. But it must have been about then.'

'We need to be precise about these things.'

'Look,' said James. 'I don't know what you're getting at, but whatever it is will you please just come out and say it. You think I've got something to do with this, don't you? You think I've hurt Lisa? You're crazy. You must be out of your mind.'

'James,' said Mrs Bellingham, putting a restraining hand on his arm. 'Calm down.'

'Calm down! Lisa's missing. We're all out of our heads with worry and now they're trying to say . . .'

'Nobody's saying anything,' the policeman insisted. 'We just need to piece together what happened. The girl's been through a lot recently. We've spoken to the psychologist she's been seeing. Apparently, the trauma of the accident brought a lot of things to the surface.'

'The psychologist brought a lot of things to the surface, you mean,' said James. 'She's been digging it all up. That's why Lisa was upset. That's what she was telling us about. If I was you, it'd be her lunatic of a mother I was questioning. I mean, when did she first report Lisa missing?'

'This morning.'

'This morning!' sneered James. 'If one of us — even me at nearly eighteen — didn't turn up home one night, Mum'd be on the phone straight away. She wouldn't wait till the next flaming morning.'

'Apparently Lisa's mother had got a bit wound up about the row, put the twins to bed and taken some sedatives. Then on top of that she'd had a couple of whiskies. Fell asleep in the chair. Didn't wake up till the early hours and assumed Lisa had come home and gone to bed. It wasn't until this morning that she discovered the bed hadn't been slept in.'

'Sounds like a pack of lies to me,' said James. 'She's completely neurotic about Lisa. She'd have checked whether she was in. I reckon Lisa went home, they had another row . . .'

'Possible,' said the policeman. 'If I'm lucky this will just be another teenage runaway I'm dealing with. Nothing more sinister.'

James grabbed hold of Kits' chair, as the police officers left, wheeled it into her room and slammed the door shut.

'Did you see?' he asked. 'Did you see the way he looked at me when he said he hoped it was nothing more sinister?'

'I don't think he meant anything. I mean he couldn't possibly think . . .'

'He could and he does,' said James.

'And what about you?' said Kits. 'What do you think? You don't really believe she had a row with her mum and walked out, do you?'

'Why not?' said James. 'It seems the most likely . . .'

'No,' said Kits. 'It's not that. I know it's not. She'd have come here. Phoned, at least. She'd have been in touch by now.'

'So, what then?' said James. 'What's happened to her?'

Kits shook her head.

'How come you don't know?' James snapped. 'If you're so good with your premonitions, how come you don't know what's happened to her?'

'I don't know,' Kits yelled at him. 'Do you think I haven't tried? I've been trying all flaming day. Looking at photos of Lisa. Holding the CD she bought me for my birthday. Trying to feel something, sense something, see something. But it doesn't work like that. It doesn't work to order, James. I'm not sure what it is. Why it is. How it happens. But it doesn't work to order.'

'You've got to make it work,' said James. 'Think! How do you get the feelings, how . . .'

'You're not listening!' said Kits. 'I've just told you. I've no idea! I've done all kinds of things. Things I haven't told any of you about. But they're only little things, really. When I was playing . . . experimenting . . . before the fire dream . . . before I got scared . . . I tried guessing the lottery numbers. I mean, if you're psychic, why not go for something really useful, like a couple of million. But it didn't work. Then the next day, I get this funny feeling. That there's something soft and furry touching me all the time. And then Lewis comes in with that guinea pig his friend gave him and dumps it on my knee. Big deal. Girl predicts arrival of guinea pig. If it's real, if it's anything more than random coincidence, it's only useless bits of trivia.'

'Not all of it. It was you who got me round to Lisa's in the first place. What if that was real precognition? What if you were sensing mega trouble? The trouble she's in now, rather than the ongoing bother with her mum and the business in the past . . . ?'

'What if? What if?' Kits repeated. 'What good does it do? Whatever I sensed then, I can't sense now. What do you want me to do, James? Throw myself into some sort of trance? Get my crystal ball out? Pack of Tarot cards perhaps?'

'Just think,' said James. 'Think for a minute. What you told me before. You told me you felt Lisa was frightened. Terrified, you said.'

'Yes. Of an eagle. But I don't think I'll bother telling the police that she might have been whisked off by a giant bird of prey.'

'No but it still might mean something. Like Mum said. A symbol.'

'Of what?'

'I don't know. It might be worth looking up. You can get books about dream symbols.'

'Well, while you're looking, check out something else. I was going to tell you the other day, when Mum interrupted. What I saw . . . what I kept seeing . . . what I saw again last night . . . was Lisa and the eagle and a lamb, sitting down. A green lamb.'

'A green lamb,' James repeated. 'Sitting down.'

'I know. I told you. It's crazy. But that's what I saw . . . I thought, at first, the lamb might be Jesus. I mean, I know we're not particularly religious but I thought the lamb might be a symbol of Jesus . . . protecting her . . . see? But I couldn't figure out why it was green.'

'No,' said James. 'It doesn't make much sense, does it? Wasn't there anything more definite? Any sense of time or place . . . ?'

'No,' said Kits, trying not to shout in frustration. 'And now I don't see or feel anything except my own panic. It's like I'm too close. Too wrapped up in it all.'

She flopped back, her head resting on her chair. James stood up. Paced up and down the room.

'I can't even do that,' she said. 'I can't even pace. I'm stuck in this bloody chair. Totally bloody useless. What are we going to do, James? What are we going to do?'

There was nothing they could do. Only wait. Wait for a phone call. A knock on the door. Lie in their beds, waiting. Sleep impossible.

Kits had got used to not sleeping, since the accident. But this was different. She felt sick. Physically sick. She propped herself up on the pillows, trying not to retch. Lisa was out there. Somewhere. There were police out there, still looking. Checking Lisa's friends. Door-to-door local searches. They were doing everything they could. That's what they said. But would it be enough? Lisa might not even be . . . No. She wouldn't allowed herself to think that way. Lisa was alive.

Then why hadn't she been in touch? Where was she? Where had she gone? Where was she hiding? And what, if anything, did visions of eagles and lambs have to do with it?

Kits slithered down the bed and lay quite still. Dare she try it? Dare she try the out-of-body thing again? Since the last, dismal time, she'd been to the school library. They didn't have much but she'd managed to find a few books. *Men and Mystery*, *Strange but True*, and *The Real X Files*. She'd skipped the chapters on UFOs, alien abduction and sightings of the Loch Ness Monster, to find what she wanted. It was all there. Pages and pages of 'evidence' about prediction and extrasensory perception. But could you believe it? Or were they all frauds? Nutters?

What had particularly interested her were the chapters on out-of-body experience or astral travelling, as a couple of books described it. There were dozens of cases, documented. The most convincing were the Indian Fakirs who claimed to be able to do it at will. From what she had read, they seemed quite comfortable with it. As if it were no more bizarre than catching a bus. There was no mention of fear, or things going wrong. But then, they'd worked on it, meditated, developed it as a life skill. Whereas she'd had it dumped on her. A side effect of the accident or hospital treatment. The result of a damaged brain, perhaps?

How could you trust it? How did James expect her to play around with something she couldn't understand, let alone control? And if she were to try it? Just one more time. What guarantee did she have? It probably wouldn't lead her to Lisa at all. She'd end up witnessing a plane crash, a murder or some other horror she didn't want to see.

Then again, it might not work at all. Not after she'd been so scared. Her fear would hold her back, for sure. She couldn't let go. Not even for Lisa. Could she? She forced her eyes shut. Relax. That was the key. Focus. Wait and see. Feel the heaviness of the body give way to lightness. It didn't have to be scary. This freedom — that's what it was. Freedom. Freedom from the paralysis that trapped her body. She didn't have to be trapped. Not if she wasn't scared. Not if she let go.

It felt good. As if all her worries had been left down there. In her body. On the bed.

CHAPTER ELEVEN

Lisa moved slowly, edging along the damp walls, touching them with her fingertips. It was dark now. Pitch-black. But she knew the layout of the room. Knew it was empty. There was nothing to stumble against. She'd taken in every detail of the bare, grey walls earlier, when light from the tiny, boarded-up window had given faint illumination to her prison.

She hadn't been able to see through the cracks in the boards. The window was too high up. She'd been blindfolded on the journey. She had no idea where she was. Or how far away from home. She sensed the echoing neglect of a large, derelict building of some sort. Possibly near water. Or maybe it was just the rain she remembered. It had been raining last night. Maybe it was still raining. She thought she could hear it raining.

She could move around freely though her hands were tied behind her back and her mouth gagged. Strangely she felt calmer now, alone in the dark. Help would come. She was sure of it, had forced herself to be sure.

Her mother would have reported her missing. When? How long would she have waited? Not long. How long would it have taken for the police to start treating it seriously? Lots of teenage girls stayed out overnight. Some ran away. She wished now that she hadn't said those stupid things to James about leaving home. Maybe they'd think she'd simply absconded. Maybe they wouldn't bother searching at all.

No. They'd be searching all right. And if they were clever, they'd find her. They'd find out who'd brought her here. They had to.

Lisa leant against the walls, trying not to shake. Not to fall. Thoughts of him shattered all pretended calm. The hunger, cold, exhaustion, fear were crowding in on her again. Just as they'd done last night.

She'd been so stupid. Broken all the rules. Ignored all the warnings and advice she'd ever been given. Like never walk home alone. Why had she insisted that James drop her off? And, when he did, why hadn't she gone straight home? Facing her mother's hysteria could be nothing to this. But she'd got as far as the front gate. Had actually opened it. Maybe even stepped onto the path, before changing her mind.

She'd been crazy. Walking round the streets alone. In the rain. Not even concentrating. Head down, thinking about Kits, about James, about

Toby, her mother, the psychologist, the accident . . . She'd meant to go home. In time. She hadn't intended to stay out all night. She'd just needed a bit of time and space.

She'd been so busy thinking, fretting, that she hadn't even heard the car draw up, further down the street. Hadn't seen anyone get out. She hadn't known he was there until he loomed right in front of her.

Lisa pressed back hard against the wall, forcing herself to breathe. Deep breaths, not the shallow ones which caught in her throat, threatening to choke her. She had never known that breathing could be so difficult. It was supposed to come naturally. Not as a battle, with your heart drumming against your ribs, your temples threatening to explode.

She should have screamed. Run off. As soon as she saw him standing there. Stranger danger and all that. Except that he wasn't a stranger. She'd heard some statistics once which she couldn't quite remember. Some ridiculously high percentage of victims knowing their assailants. Their murderers. People they knew. People they'd open their doors to. People they trusted.

Well, she hadn't trusted Ross. But she'd fallen straight into the trap. Instead of running away, the minute she saw him, she'd actually stood there and spoken to him.

'What are you doing here?'

She'd really said that. Stupid. Corny. Crazy. But she'd said it.

'I've been to see your mother,' he'd answered, as though it was the most natural thing in the world. 'She was in a right state. You not being home. Out with some lad, she said. I said I'd look out for you on my way home.'

'Home?' Lisa had repeated. 'I thought you were still in . . .'

'I'm out now. Don't bother counting up. Nobody does full time. I've got a place I'm renting.'

'Fine. But stay away from us, OK. Mum doesn't want anything to do with you. There's a court order. You're not allowed to come near.'

'Your mum's changed her mind. Didn't she tell you? Didn't she tell you about coming to see me? Very touching it was. Visiting time in the nick. In the afternoons, when you were safe at school.'

'That's not true.'

'Isn't it? You didn't think she'd give me up, did you? Not really?'

Lisa had hesitated. It was possible. Mum was completely screwed up. Who could tell what she'd do?

'We're going to be OK, this time. Your mum knows that. I've been having treatment. Inside. I don't drink no more. And I've done courses. On

130

handling aggression. They wouldn't have let me out so soon if I hadn't done so well with my lessons, now would they?'

'I don't believe you. I don't believe a word of this,' Lisa had yelled.

A woman, with a dog, on the other side of the street had paused, looked at them, as Ross had put his hand on her arm.

Why hadn't she screamed out then? Why had she let the woman walk on? Because she was already hooked. Caught up in what Ross was saying.

'You don't have to take my word. Ask your mum. Come on. We'll go 'n' ask her together. See what she says, eh?'

It was like enticing toddlers with sweets. As easy as that. She'd got into the car, desperation blinding common sense. Desperation to prove it wasn't true, obliterating everything she'd ever been told. She remembered it all now. The leaflets. The talks at school. About how clever some of these perverts were. Telling kids they'd got a puppy in the car. Or pretending to be police officers. Or saying someone had had an accident.

Ross hadn't needed to bother with anything so tricky. Just get in the car, Lisa, and we'll go and ask your mum. He'd kept her talking. Taunting her with his renewed relationship with her mother, so it had taken her a good five minutes to realize they were going the wrong way.

By then, it was too late. He'd got it all planned out. Driving into a back alley, with high fences, where no-one would see. Holding a knife to her throat.

She'd thought she was going to die there and then. But no. He'd taped her mouth, tied her hands and put a scarf round her eyes.

He was still talking as he drove off. She couldn't answer. Couldn't reason, even if she'd known what to say.

'You see, Lisa, I've come back. You knew I would, didn't you? You knew I wouldn't let you get away with it. I thought I'd messed it up before. I thought they'd come looking for me but they didn't. So I thought to myself, she doesn't know. Lisa doesn't know.'

Lisa had shaken her head, partly in a vain attempt to be rid of the gag and partly to indicate that she had no idea what he was talking about.

'But it's been bugging me, see?' Ross went on. 'I was sure you'd seen me. I meant you to. I meant to stop – real close – just to give you a fright. But that girl you were with, she spooked me, leaping around, like she did . . . I couldn't stop.'

The gag stopped Lisa from crying out as she suddenly knew what he was talking about. Momentarily saw it flash before her blindfolded eyes. The car. The headlights. The driver.

Kits had been right. In the split second, as that

car came towards them, Lisa had seen the face of the driver. Recognized Ross. Had frozen. If she hadn't, if her reflexes had been as quick as Kits', would they both have made it, out of the way? Had her hesitation stopped Kits from following her to safety? Was that the guilt she'd tried to bury?

Or was it worse than that? Was it the knowledge that she, herself, had been the target? Not Kits. Kits became the victim because she was there. Wrong place. Wrong time. Wrong person.

'I know. I know,' he'd said as Lisa writhed in her seat. 'Your mate got hurt bad. But it weren't my fault. I never meant to hurt her. I lay low for a while. I kept expecting the cops to come snooping. But they didn't. And I think, why hasn't Lisa told them? She must have seen me. It's not like my Lisa to miss a chance to get me sent down again. That's when I started following you.'

Lisa's muscles had gone rigid, as her mind grappled with the possibility. Had he been following her? Hadn't she known? Hadn't she seen? How long could it have been going on?

'When I saw you going to that head doctor, that shrink, I sorta put two and two together. She don't remember now, I thought. But she will. Soon enough. In't that right, Lisa?'

She hadn't been able to answer the question. Hadn't been able to speak until he'd dragged her

133

up here, removed the blindfold and, for a while, the tape.

'So it was all lies?' she said. 'You haven't seen Mum? She's not having you back?'

'You're so thick aren't you? Have me back? She'd kill me if she saw me again. You ruined everything for me, you did.'

'So how did you find us? How did you know? Mum's been so careful.'

'Are you kidding? You can't keep nothin' secret these days. Every detail. Every move yer make's logged on a hundred computers. I've watched you going back and forwards from school. I've kept an eye on the house. Saw the boyfriend turn up. Followed you to his house and back to yours. You see, it's not difficult to find someone, Lisa. It's knowing what to do with them, when you've got 'em, that's the problem.'

'So why do it? Why bring me here? I wouldn't have said anything. I couldn't. I'd blocked it out. I didn't know. I didn't know.'

'And now you do. Pity.'

'Please . . .'

'Don't try that, Lisa. Not the pleading. I might lose my temper, see?'

'I thought you'd had classes for that,' Lisa snapped, before she could stop herself.

'I did. That bit were true. You get out quicker if you play the reform game. And they helped.

134

They really did help. I'm not gonna do anything hasty, see. I'm in control. In a day or two, maybe a week, they'll find a body in the canal. A teenage runaway who stumbled in the dark and fell, maybe . . .'

'You're mad,' Lisa had screamed at him.

'Am I?' Ross had said, moving up close so she could feel his breath, hot and putrid. 'Mad enough to do it?'

The memories made her weak. She slid down and crouched, knees drawn up to her chest, on the cold floor. He'd laughed as he'd walked out. He hadn't been back. Did he mean to leave her here? Tied up. Gagged. Helpless. Waiting to die of starvation. Exhaustion. Before he dumped her body.

At first, when he'd left, she'd tried throwing herself against the door, in the hope of forcing it open, or making enough noise to alert someone. But the door was secure and there was nobody around to hear. Her shoulders sore and bruised, she had decided to stop. To conserve her energy, in case a real chance of escape presented itself. In case he came back.

What would be worse? Ross coming back? She could still feel the cold embrace of the knife pressed against her throat. Or not coming back? Of nobody coming here ever again?

She realized she was rocking backwards and forwards, crying again. She had cried so much she barely knew she was doing it, until her eyes began to sting and her throat ached.

She felt the tears run down her face and tasted their salt on the edge of her mouth, where the gag cut into her lips. She tried the breaths again. Deep. Through her nose. Tried singing. Not out loud, of course, but in her head. Music she'd listened to with Kits. Music which made her happy.

It was working. She was calming down again. Almost. Until she heard the footsteps. One set of footsteps. He was back. She was sure it was him. No rescuer would come alone.

Lisa pushed herself against the wall, scrambling to her feet as the door opened. He'd brought the torch again. There had been a torch, last night. A torch and a knife.

No knife now. At least not in his hand. He moved towards her, pointing the torch low, so as not to blind her eyes. Thoughtful.

'You're quite famous now, Lisa,' he said. 'Been on the news and everything.'

He pulled the gag from her mouth.

'Now don't scream or try anything, 'cos that would be silly. There's no-one to hear and it would make me mad, OK?'

Lisa nodded. What was she supposed to do? Just stand here, quietly, letting him do whatever it was he'd decided to do? There must come a point when you had to fight back. But when? How? She could kick. Bite. But what good would that do with her hands still tied?

'I might hurt you if I got mad,' he said, circling her, forcing her to turn with him, watching every move. 'It doesn't have to hurt, you know. I can make it quick, painless . . . if I wanted to. I killed someone before, you know.'

'No!' Lisa said, hoping it wasn't true, not wanting to know.

'Someone who made me mad,' he said, as if justifying it to himself. 'It was her own fault. I warned her not to say them things to me. She shouldn't have said what she did . . .'

Lisa lowered her eyes. She didn't want to look at him. She didn't want to hear this new confession. The more she knew, the more reason he'd have . . .

'They never found her. But they'll find you. Eventually. When they start searching the canal. Poor Lisa. Was it suicide? Was it an accident? There'll be nothing to connect it to me,' he said, smiling to himself. 'I'll have to do it, you know. I couldn't just let you go. Not now you know so much. You do see that, don't you, Lisa?'

Answer him. Talk. Keep him talking. Lisa knew that was her only chance, but her lips, her vocal chords, refused to respond to the message from her brain. His very presence made her paralysed. She tried flexing her fingers. Nothing. All feelings drained, first from her body and then her mind.

There was no longer any panic. Any fear. Only emptiness. Acceptance. She was already dead.

His sudden movement jolted her. Every centimetre of her body jerked into action as if she'd been hurled against an electric fence. She bolted to the far corner of the room.

Only then did she realize that Ross hadn't been moving towards her. He was moving towards the door, tense and anxious.

'Did you hear that?' he said. 'Did you see it?'

Lisa nodded, though she had seen and heard nothing.

'There are no ghosts,' he said, staring around, wide-eyed. 'There are no ghosts. Are there, Lisa?'

Lisa shook her head, terrified to speak, Terrified of making a mistake.

'But she comes, you know,' he said, his eyes fixed on the far wall. 'She's here now.'

Lisa shuddered. He was crazy. Seriously crazy. If he'd been a bit unhinged before, he was now seriously deranged.

His eyes flicked round the room, as if watching someone. Something. Drawn in by Ross's para-noia, she began to shiver, imagining a cold, ghostly presence in the room. The girl? The one he'd killed?

Clearly that's what Ross believed. He was shaking, uncontrollably. She wondered, fleetingly, whether he was on drugs. Hallucinating.

It didn't matter. He seemed to have lost all interest in her. He backed out of the room. Slamming the door shut. Pausing to fasten the bolts. Leaving her in the dark. With the ghost.

CHAPTER TWELVE

Ross had gone but Lisa could sense that she wasn't alone. Her legs buckled beneath her. She sank back onto the cold floor, not in fear but in relief. Ghosts held no terror for her. The living were more dangerous than the dead and she'd had a reprieve. There was hope.

Her hands were still tied, the door still bolted. But, in his panic. Ross hadn't replaced the gag. Her mouth, though sore and parched, was free.

Lisa's instinct was to cry out, immediately. But no. She bit into her lip, making it bleed. Anything to stifle the sound which threatened to erupt. She would wait. Wait a long time. Make sure that he was well away from the building. Then, when the first light began to show through the boarded window, she would scream. Carry on screaming until someone heard her.

And someone would hear her. She was sure of that. It was almost as though someone had already heard her silent screams and had wrapped a blanket of warm, protective calm around her.

Her mind played with the idea of rescue, imagining hundreds of possible scenes, until her eyes began to close. She tried to force them open. To stay alert. Stay awake. But a heavy weight was pressing them shut.

In the hazy no-man's-land between waking and sleep, she felt the ghost departing.

She heard words. But who said them? Was it Ross as he slammed the door? Or was it the ghost? Somebody had said them. They rolled across her mind like waves on the shore.

'I'll be back. I'll be back.'

The scream rang out. Only one scream. Continuous. Infinite. As though it was the last and only sound left in the universe.

The door burst open. Lewis rushed in, followed by Mr Bellingham. Mrs Bellingham. James.

Kits lay on the bed, writhing, screaming. Her dad rushed over, holding her, supporting her in his arms, until the screaming finally stopped.

'James, phone the doc . . .'

'No,' said Kits. 'No. The police. I want the police.'

'Why?' said James. 'What's hap . . . ?'

'I've seen Lisa,' Kits said, her voice shrill, hysterical.

'Oh, no,' said Mrs Bellingham. 'Kits, please. Please don't. It's hard enough . . . It was a dream, love. Another dream.'

'They're not dreams,' Kits screamed. 'I can leave my body. Like I did during the operation. I've been there. I saw her. There was someone with her.'

'Been where, Kits?' said James.

'Oh, for goodness' sake, don't encourage her,' Mrs Bellingham snapped. 'Can't you see she's ill?'

'I don't know,' said Kits, ignoring the interruption. 'A big building. Huge. Empty. Not far. He's keeping her there.'

'He? Who?' questioned Mr Bellingham, avoiding his wife's eyes.

'I don't know. I don't always see things that clear. Just shapes. Images. Feelings, like . . .'

'Like a dream,' her dad said, gently.

'No. It was real. He sensed me. They both sensed me, though not strongly. He was frightened, like I was a ghost or something.'

'Get dressed, James. Get the car out,' said Mrs Bellingham, starting to cry. 'I'm taking Kits up to the hospital.'

James looked at the clock on the mantelpiece. 4:24 a.m.

'What are you looking at that for?' said his mother. 'What does it matter what time it is?'

James shrugged, helplessly. He didn't know why he'd looked. It just seemed important to know. And now he did, what should he do? Kits didn't need medical treatment. There was nothing wrong with her, in that sense. Somehow she'd done what he'd asked her to do. And now he had to do his bit. He had to make his parents believe her.

'What if she's right?' he blurted out. 'She's been right before. Too often to be coincidence.'

Mr Bellingham touched his wife's arm, trying to prevent the screamed response he felt sure was coming.

'Even if she is,' Mr Bellingham mused, 'what have we got to go on? A vague idea of a building . . . a person.'

'Those other dreams,' said James. 'The eagle. The green lamb. Maybe, put together, it all means something.'

'It means Kits is ill,' said Mrs Bellingham. 'The accident. Lisa disappearing. We don't know what it's doing to her. And we're standing here, wasting time, talking about supernatural claptrap.'

'What's all this about a lamb?' said Lewis. 'I didn't know about that. What else has she seen?'

'Does it matter?' Mrs Bellingham snapped.

'It might . . .' Lewis began.

'No, Lewis, it doesn't,' Mrs Bellingham insisted. 'All that matters is getting Kits to a doctor. Don't you understand? She's sick.'

'OK,' said Kits. 'I'm sick. Mad. Loopy. Deranged. I'll see a doctor. Talk to a psychologist. Have a brain scan. Whatever you want. But we phone the police first.'

'And say what?' said Mr Bellingham. 'Think

143

about it, love. The police aren't going to believe . . .'

'Maybe not,' said Kits. 'But I've got to try. I'm not going anywhere until I've spoken to them. Just get them here, OK. And I'll do the rest.'

Mr Bellingham made no mention of dreams when he made the phone call. Just that they had remembered something. Something that might help in the Lisa Mountjoy case. And, no, he wasn't prepared to discuss it over the phone.

The genuine anxiety in his voice had obviously done the trick. Two officers arrived within the hour. A lady, whom they had met before in connection with the hit-and-run, and a senior policeman, called Willis.

Neither of them questioned why the Bellinghams were all up and dressed, sitting round the kitchen table, drinking tea, at five thirty in the morning. They didn't even ask why, precisely they had been summoned, or what the family may have remembered. They simply accepted tea and Willis brought out a photograph.

'I was going to come round later this morning, anyway,' he said.

He pushed the photograph towards James.

'Do you recognize him?'

James looked. Shook his head.

'Sure?' said the policeman, passing it to James's

144

parents. 'Bit of a long shot. Thought you might have seen him hanging around recently.'

Mr and Mrs Bellingham shook their heads and passed it to Kits. She grabbed it, irritably. She didn't want to be looking at photographs. She wanted to talk. Tell him what she knew. Make him believe her.

She glanced down. Head and shoulders shot. Adult. Male. Kits gasped, as she touched it.

'You know him?' said the police officer, hopefully.

'No. Not really. I got . . . I felt . . .'

'Kits hasn't been too well,' said her mother, hastily. 'Since the accident. She gets worked up.'

As Kits passed it to Lewis, glad to be free of the strange sensation, a second photograph came towards her. Same man. Longer shot. Blue tee-shirt. You could just see the top of denim jeans. Muscular arms.

'Never mind,' said Willis, registering the blank faces. 'You said you'd remembered something though.'

'Wait,' said Kits, leaning forward, sharing the photograph with James. 'Look at that.'

'What?'

'That tattoo, on his arm. What does it look like to you?'

'A bird,' said James. 'A bird with its wings outstretched.'

145

'I can tell you what it is,' said the police officer. 'It's an . . .'

'Eagle,' said Kits.

'Who is he?' said Mrs Bellingham, pressing her hands to her temples, feeling her head was going to explode with the sheer tension and impossibility of it all.

Kits could hardly bear to listen. Alerted by what Lisa's psychologist had told them, the police had questioned Lisa's mother, again. They'd talked about the rows. About the past. About Ross. Later they'd gone over the court case. His conviction for assaulting Toby. They'd noted his recent, early release from prison. He had become a suspect.

Only that in their eyes, at the moment. A possible suspect. Like James. Kits' vision of eagles hardly counted as evidence. But she knew. She knew for certain that the hazy figure she had seen in that room last night was Lisa's stepfather, Ross.

She told the police officers about her dreams. It wasn't easy. The disbelief, pity almost, in their eyes. James's interruptions confirming that she'd been right before. Her mother's interruptions saying it was all coincidence. That Kits needed help. And, at the end of it all, watching them stand up, preparing to leave.

'You're not going to do anything, are you?' she asked. 'You don't believe me, do you?'

'It's not a case of believing,' said Willis. 'This could still turn out to be nothing more than a teenage runaway. But, just in case, we're trying to trace the whereabouts of this stepfather.'

'And if you don't find him? What then? What about Lisa? What about the building I told you about?'

'If anybody can tell me where it is,' said Willis, 'then I'll search it, whether you've seen it in a dream or a crystal ball. But there are dozens of derelict factories round here . . .'

'Search them all,' said Kits.

Before Willis could answer, the phone rang. Mr Bellingham picked it up, said a few words and passed it to Willis. He nodded and mumbled into the phone. Single words. Yes. No. Right.

'Looks like we might be right,' he said. 'We've been showing copies of the photos to Lisa's neighbours. There've been a couple of positive sightings. Including from the lady with the dog. She thinks it might have been Ross she saw with Lisa.'

'Thinks,' said Kits, gripping the arms of her chair. 'Doesn't she know?'

'It was dark, remember. She only caught a glimpse. She's pretty sure about Lisa but not the person with her. She told us, at first, that it was a girl and her boyfriend having a row. When she saw the photo, she said, yes, it might have been Ross. But she couldn't be sure.'

'She might not be,' said Kits. 'But I am. You've got to listen to me. You've got to find him. You've got to.'

'We'll find him,' said Willis. 'We're already checking out all the likely places he might be staying. Bedsits, hostels, that sort of thing. He won't be using his own name of course but . . .'

'That's it!' Lewis suddenly blurted out. 'That's what Kits' dream might mean. He might be using the name Lamb or Green. Or staying at a place with those words . . .'

He stopped. It was no use. Willis was already walking out of the door. He thought the whole family was crazy.

Lisa dragged herself to her feet as soon as her eyes snapped open. How long had she slept? How had she managed to sleep at all? The room was lighter. Slightly. Maybe. She couldn't be sure.

Too soon for anyone to be about? If there was ever anyone about. Without knowing exactly where she was, she couldn't be sure. Maybe the building wasn't entirely derelict. Maybe some sort of caretaker came by, sometimes. Ross must have driven right up to the building. He hadn't dragged her far, once they had left the car. It couldn't be far away from a road. Roads meant people.

She was wasting time. Thinking. Imagining possibilities. She moved to what she thought might be the best distance from the high window, tilted her head towards it and began to shout.

Her cries echoed, engulfing the room with their sound. But were they reaching far enough? Were they reaching outside? Was it best to shout continuously and risk collapsing with exhaustion? Or pace yourself? Take breaks. But then, someone might just be passing, in the minute that you stopped.

The thoughts throbbed in her head as she shouted. Her voice got weaker, her throat sore. Nobody came.

CHAPTER THIRTEEN

James looked at his watch as the phone rang. 9:25. He wondered why he was so obsessed with time. Time which seemed to be dragging by, unbearably slowly.

He grabbed the receiver, willing it to be news. Any news. It was the secretary at Lewis's school.

'Lew's not well,' James informed Kits as he put the phone down. 'I've got to go and get him.'

'I'm not surprised,' snapped Kits. 'I don't know why Mum insisted he went to school.'

'She's trying to keep things as normal as possible,' said James. 'We've all had so much time off already.' ·

It was true, Kits thought, as James went to collect Lewis. Lew had his exams, his SATS, coming up in a couple of months and Mum and Dad couldn't really afford any more time off work. Besides, Mum had pointed out, there was nothing any of them could do but wait.

So James, who had a light morning at college, had been detailed to stay with Kits. Even Mum could see she was in no fit state to go to school or to be left alone.

She wished James would hurry up. The junior school was only round the corner. What was taking him so long? He would have to walk, of course. Mum and Dad had taken the cars. Even so . . .

She swung her wheelchair round as she heard the door slam. James rushed in, followed by Lewis looking very flushed.

'You OK?' Kits asked.

'Fine,' said Lewis. 'A bit wet. It's pouring down, again.'

'I don't want a weather report. I want to know about you.'

'He's not ill,' said James. 'He just pretended to be. To get out of school. He's had an idea.'

'I was in assembly,' said Lewis, babbling so fast that Kits could barely follow him. 'We were singing this hymn about the lamb of God so of course that got me thinking about your dreams and the eagle and the green lamb and we know about the eagle now on the tattoo and you've been right about nearly everything so it makes sense that the lamb has got to be involved somehow. I thought it might be a name, yeah, but . . .'

'Lewis,' Kits shouted. 'We couldn't just get to the point, could we? You're giving me a headache.'

'I've remembered where I've seen one.'

'What?' said Kits, now thoroughly bemused.

'You know the old factories along the canal?' said James, taking over. 'Well, a couple of them were wool mills, yes?'

'They made one into that craft centre,' said Kits.

'Yeah,' said Lewis. 'But further down, where I go on my bike, past the bridge, there's one that's still derelict. And there's this animal carved into the stonework. You hardly notice it now 'cos it's all worn and faded and I'm not even sure what it's supposed to be but it's lying down. And it would make sense it being a lamb . . . on a wool mill and . . .'

'Lewis says the stonework's got a sort of moss growing on it,' James finished, sensing that Kits was getting irritated by Lewis's rambling. 'It looks green. A green lamb, Kits.'

Lisa's shouts had become fainter. Less regular. She was taking longer breaks, out of necessity rather than desire. It was as light now as it ever got in the room. She could just about see the hands on her watch. 9:45. She'd been here how long? 36 hours. 36 hours that felt like a lifetime. How long could you survive without food or drink or hope?

No. Lisa shook her head. She wouldn't let herself think like that. She let her hatred for Ross burn inside her, drawing energy from its flames. Somehow, some way, she would get out. She wouldn't let them down again. Toby and Kits. Her evidence, about the hit-and-run, the kidnap, the previous murder he'd claimed to have committed, would put him away for the rest of his life. He'd never be able to hurt anyone ever again.

'Help. Help me. Help,' she screamed again at the window.

Over and over.

She stopped every few minutes to listen. To see if she could hear any response. A car stopping. A dog barking. Footsteps. Any noise to tell her that she wasn't totally alone.

Footsteps. This time she heard footsteps. Running. Getting closer. Not outside. In the building. Someone had heard her. Someone was coming to let her out. She shouted again.

'Help me. I'm Lisa. Lisa Mountjoy. Help.'

She rushed forward as the door burst open. Stopped in her tracks. Rescue had so dominated her mind that she had failed to consider the other possibility.

Only now, faced with Ross, flushed, breathless, angry, did her hopes collapse.

'That was stupid, Lisa,' he said. 'Real stupid.'

Hope gone, there was nothing left to sustain her. Ross's shape blurred in front of her eyes, the room spun round, her legs crumpled. In the instant before she lost consciousness, she saw Ross's face looming over her inert body and knew she was going to die.

*   *   *

Kits' head suddenly jerked back as the wheelchair bumped along the towpath.

'We're too late,' she screamed out. 'James, we're too late.'

James clicked on the brakes of the chair and went round to face Kits, while Lewis stared at them, helplessly.

'I saw something. Just now,' Kits said. 'In the canal.'

James looked over to the water. Lewis looked.

'No,' sobbed Kits. 'Not there. I wasn't looking at the water. It was in my head. A picture. The police. Dragging something . . . they were dragging a body out of the canal.'

James shook his head, refusing to believe. He released the brake, grabbed the handles, carried on pushing. They couldn't be too late. They couldn't.

They'd spent only a few minutes, back at the house, discussing their options. What to do with Lewis's information? Phone the police? Get their parents back from work? Risk being dismissed as crazy, again?

They'd decided to follow Lewis's suggestion to take a preliminary look before alerting anyone. At first Kits hadn't wanted to go. Pushing her wheelchair would only slow them down. Waste valuable time. But James wouldn't leave her in the house alone.

So they had made their way down to the canal.

James and Lewis had struggled to lift the chair down the steps to the towpath, pushing her along the muddy surface. It had been raining heavily for the past few days. It was raining now. Only a light drizzle but enough to discourage ramblers or dog walkers. They were quite alone. And almost there. They couldn't see the building. The bridge obscured their view. But they were close.

'It's no good,' Kits cried. 'It's over. We're too late.'

'We don't know that,' James insisted. 'What do you expect me to do? Give up? Turn back?'

Suddenly the sheer madness of it all hit him. He'd been crazy to listen to Lewis. Lewis was only a kid. This wasn't some Famous Five adventure. They couldn't do it on their own.

'Lewis,' James said. 'You have to go back. Now. Phone the police. Tell them where we are. Get them here.'

'They won't listen to me,' Lewis wailed. 'What am I supposed to say?'

'Say your crazy crippled sister's down at the canal,' said Kits, immediately realizing James was right. 'Don't mention that James is with me. Say you can't get me to go home. Say anything. Just make sure they come, OK?'

Lewis nodded and raced off. James carried on pushing Kits as quickly as he could towards the bridge. Towards the building.

Kits heard the footsteps first. Heavy footsteps pounding behind them, as they reached the bridge. Alerted by his sister, James swung round.

'Keys,' Lewis yelled continuing to bound towards them. 'House keys, James. I need the house keys.'

'Hurry up!' Kits pleaded as the keys were handed over. 'Don't gawp after him, James, push.'

Once under the bridge, the building came into view. Six storeys high. Broken or boarded-up windows.

'Look,' said James, swinging Kits' chair around to face it. 'Look up there. The animal carved into the stonework.'

Kits peered up. It was very faint. Green with moss, as Lewis had said. Barely noticeable. Goodness knows how he'd ever spotted it in the first place or come to remember it. But it was a lamb. Her legs might not work but her eyesight was perfect. It was definitely a lamb.

'Can you see a way in?' said Kits. 'There's no sign of a door or . . .'

'I think there might have been once,' said James. 'It's been bricked up. See where the bricks are a different colour?'

'We've come the wrong way,' said Kits, urgently. 'We're wasting time. There must be a way in, round the back. There must be some sort of entrance from the road.'

'I've never noticed one,' said James. 'But maybe you wouldn't. Not unless you were looking. How about if we shout? Maybe if we shout her name?'

'No,' said Kits. 'Wait.'

Her eyes suddenly blazed with a brightness, an animation, James hadn't seen since the accident.

'She's there,' said Kits. 'She's there, James. She's still OK. But I don't think she's alone.'

'Aren't you sure? Can't you tell?'

'I'm not Mystic flaming Meg, you know,' Kits snapped. 'I'm sorry. But you know what it's like. I've told you. It's not always clear. But I can sense her. I know she's there.'

'We could go back . . . try to find our way from the road . . .'

'It'd take ages,' said Kits, anxiously. 'We can't risk it. And besides I think there's a way. Push me a bit further.'

James pushed, tense and alert, listening, looking for any signs of movement.

'Look,' said Kits as they reached the end of the building. 'There's a gap between the building and the wall. A few bushes in the way but . . .'

'I can't get your chair through that gap, bushes or no bushes,' James said.

'Not me, idiot. You. You can get round easy enough.'

'Oh, no,' said James. 'I'm not leaving you here, on your own.'

157

'I'll be OK.'

The word no was on James's lips when they heard the scream.

He was slapping her face over and over. Lisa had no idea how long Ross had been doing it before he got a response. Before her eyes opened and she cried out. Immediately the gag was tied round her mouth and Lisa was dragged to her feet.

'They're on to me,' he told her. 'They've been snooping round the place I was staying . . . I got out the back, quick. I don't know how they got onto me. Maybe your mother said summat. But they're looking for me and you and me are getting out of here, Lisa. Lucky I didn't do nothing hasty eh? They won't touch me while I've got you.'

Lisa felt so weak, so sick, she could barely make sense of the words. She was only on her feet because he was holding her. Dragging her out of the room.

'I've got another car,' he said. 'And once we're away from here, I'll dump it . . . dump you . . . and then I'll disappear.'

James froze as he saw the car. Blue Ford. Driver's door left open. You didn't have to be traumatized or particularly psychic to get feelings. Sometimes you just knew.

He had only heard the one scream. The scream which had sent him tearing through the bushes and

158

along the side of the building. Here to the yard, round the back.

He rushed towards the door. Pushed it. Pulled it. Kicked it. Hurled himself at it. It didn't make any difference. It was locked.

There must be an entrance somewhere. Lisa was in there. Ross must be in there as well. James's eyes scanned the building. There was a window, low down. Broken but not boarded. He took of his jacket, wrapped it round his arm and smashed the remaining glass. He shook his jacket, put it back on and climbed in.

The jagged remains of the window tore through his trousers. His legs and hands were bleeding but he barely felt any pain. He was too busy trying to focus his eyes in the dim interior. Trying to work out where to go, what to do. The building was vast. The room he was in was about four times the size of the main hall at college. There were three doors. Three separate exits. Which one to choose? Lisa could be anywhere.

The decision was made for him. The first door he tried was locked. The second was open. He didn't bother with the third. At least an open door was progress.

He quickly scanned the new room. Smaller than the first. Two doors. He pushed one open, feeling a blast of cold, damp air. This was the door that led outside, the one Ross might have used. He closed

159

it. Tried the next. It led to a narrow stairway.

James stopped. Listened for any sound which might direct him. Anything to tell him he was on the right track. Nothing at first. Then a faint noise. Impossible to tell what it was but it was something.

He started to move up the stairs. Slowly at first, then more quickly as the noise became louder. It was footsteps. Two sets. One clear and firm. The other more muted, as if . . . as if someone were being dragged along.

He saw them as he reached the next flight of stairs. They were at the top. If James hadn't known, he'd have thought Ross was holding a life-size rag doll or a puppet. Lisa's head hung down. She seemed totally unaware of her surroundings. She hadn't seen him but Ross had.

His first expression, of total shock, quickly gave way to one of recognition.

'I know you,' he said. 'You're Lisa's boyfriend. You were with her. Look at this, Lisa. A knight in shining armour to the rescue.'

James didn't put him right about being Lisa's boyfriend and the words had absolutely no meaning to Lisa. Her head and body went where they were pushed and pulled. Her eyes were blurred, unfocused.

'How the hell did you find me?' Ross snarled.

James didn't answer. Didn't think. His body took

over, fuelled with a burning anger he couldn't control. He bounded up the stairs.

It wasn't what Ross expected. Instinctively he swung Lisa round so she was directly in front of him. Gripped her with one arm, while he reached into his pocket with the other. But before he could arm himself, he heard the screech of tyres. James heard it. Even Lisa heard it, squirming, trying to pull herself out of Ross's reach. As she lurched forward, Ross let go, sending Lisa sprawling down the stairs.

CHAPTER FOURTEEN

Fortunately James was only five stairs down from Lisa when she fell. His arms went out. Caught her. Held her close, desperately trying to keep his balance, as Ross pushed past them.

The screech of the tyres had reassured James. Lewis had managed to get the police. They would stop Ross far better than he could do. He had a moment to concentrate on Lisa. Lowering her into a sitting position on the stair, he removed the gag and the rope which bound her wrists. He noticed the gashes where the ropes had cut, the bruises on her face where Ross had hit her, the dullness of her eyes, the uncontrollable trembling.

She was in no fit state to move. No state to be left either. But James couldn't stay still. He was desperate to get outside. To find Kits. To make sure the police had got Ross.

He lifted Lisa up. It always looked easy when people did it in films. Lisa was slim but her body felt like a sack of bricks as he struggled downstairs, using his full weight to push open the door.

He almost crashed into a police officer, who helped get Lisa into the back of a car, until they could get an ambulance. James tried to take in the scene but it was too chaotic. Cars. Police cars which had stopped. More cars arriving. His dad's car. A police van with dogs. An ambulance. His mother's car. People all scurrying around, apparently without direction. Uniformed people. People he knew. People he didn't know. Willis. Willis was standing in front of him.

'Where is he?' James demanded. 'Did you get him, did . . . ?'

'Not yet, but he won't get far. Don't worry . . .'

'Where's Kits? Where's my sister? Is anyone with Kits? And Lewis. I haven't seen Lewis.'

'We told your brother to stay at home,' said Willis.

'He didn't though,' said Mrs Bellingham, coming up to join them. 'I called home to pick him up after he phoned work but he'd gone . . .'

'He'll be cycling along the towpath,' said James, 'And Kits is still there. With that lunatic on the loose.'

'It's all right,' said Willis. 'I've sent people . . .'

But he was talking to himself. James had gone.

James scrambled through the gap along the side of the building and began battling his way through the wet undergrowth. A hand grabbed him as he parted the last bush and clambered up onto the path.

Another arm grabbed him as he tried to struggle free. Clamped between two young police officers, James stared at the scene which confronted him.

Kits' chair was more or less where he had left it. But someone was behind it, holding the chair in one hand and a knife in the other.

'Don't move, don't say anything,' one of the police officers hissed at James, before releasing his arm.

'We've got to do something,' James hissed back, as Ross began to back off, dragging Kits' chair away from them, along the path in the direction of their home.

'Steady,' said one officer, putting a restraining arm on James, as the other officer edged forward, alone. 'We got here seconds after he grabbed her. We've been talking to him. If we can . . .'

'No further,' Ross yelled.

'Let the girl go,' said the officer, slowing almost, but not quite, to a halt.

'I said, no further!'

'It's all right,' said Kits, quietly.

Her face was pale, her fists clenched, but her eyes were clear, focused but somehow distant. She had moved objects before, she told herself. OK, maybe not with someone holding onto them but it couldn't be too difficult. Knives. Wheelchairs. They were easy game.

Game. That was it. Don't want it too much. Don't try too hard. Ease up. Relax. Treat it as a game.

It was already beginning to work. Her mind forcing the wheelchair to resist, was slowing Ross down. He was still trying to drag the chair backwards, checking the brakes, checking for ruts in the path, becoming frustrated when he found no apparent obstacles.

Kits could sense his frustration, turned his lack of concentration against him. She'd seen the knife, briefly. Imagined it now, pulling away from his hand. Because Ross was behind her, she had no way of knowing whether it was working.

James saw, though. The policemen saw, but had no explanation for Ross's bizarre behaviour. He was looking down at the knife which seemed to be twitching in his grasp. Then, he let go of the wheelchair, passing the knife from hand to hand, as if it was burning him. The knife dropped to the ground. Keeping his eyes on the group in front of him, Ross quickly bent to pick it up, clutching it in both hands. His hands, still holding the knife, seemed to shoot up into the air, before releasing it with incredible force.

To the policemen, it appeared that Ross had thrown it at them. They dragged James to one side, ducking as it hurtled towards them.

As the knife fell, harmlessly, onto the towpath,

they looked up to see Ross spinning the wheelchair round and round. Or was it the chair that was spinning Ross? He didn't look like a man who was in control.

Beyond the hedge, dogs started to bark. Two more officers appeared. As they did, Ross finally let go of the chair, turned and ran.

James barely noticed him. He only saw the chair, veering towards the water. Hitting a stone. Bouncing. Hurling Kits forward into the cold depths of the canal. In an instant he knew what Kits had seen, in her last vision. Not Lisa's body being dragged from the canal. But her own. Summoning what little presence of mind he had left, he kicked off his shoes, discarded his jacket and dived in.

Lewis cursed his bike, urging it to go faster. He didn't know what he was doing. He just wanted to be there. With Kits and James and his parents. That idiot Willis had told him to stay home. Well, he'd stayed long enough to phone his parents at work. Anything more was impossible.

His legs ached from running and cycling. He knew the slow progress was down to him rather than the bike and redoubled his efforts as he saw the bridge up ahead.

Someone was running towards him. No. Not one person. Three. The two at the back, police officers, seemed to be gaining ground on the one in

166

front. Ross. This had to be Ross. But where was Lisa and what about James and Kits?

Lewis pedalled faster. He didn't know why exactly or what he thought he was going to do. Maybe cut the guy off. Distract him. Delay him. Swerve round him.

The scene in front of him was becoming more crowded, more chaotic as he steered towards it. More police officers running. Reinforcements. Dogs. Two alsatians racing past the policemen. Drawing level with the officer in front, lurching at Ross. Bringing him down.

Lewis's whole body went limp with relief. Too limp to steer. Too limp to pedal. The bike seemed to fold and crumple beneath him and he slumped to the ground.

Lewis didn't know what hurt most. His head, his arm or his back which a policeman accidentally kicked in the scramble to drag Ross to his feet and handcuff him. Lewis could hear the dogs panting. Could feel their hot breath. He vaguely hoped they were back on their leashes and under control.

'Are you OK?' someone was asking.

He didn't answer. Barely listened, in fact. Another conversation in the background had caught his attention.

'What about the girl?' an officer was anxiously asking his colleague. 'The one in the wheelchair? Is she safe? Did they get her out of the canal?'

167

James was an excellent swimmer. He could swim for miles without tiring. He'd been tipped out of canoes into freezing water. Been thrown about in waves, while learning to surf. But he'd never faced anything like this. His life-saving techniques had been learnt in the safety of the swimming baths. Not here in the dark, cold waters of the canal with weeds clinging to him and grimy pollution threatening to choke him.

It could only have been a matter of seconds but it seemed like hours before his hands made contact. Kits' arms were thrashing but stopped as he grabbed her and began to kick towards the surface.

There was another figure in the water. One of the policemen from the towpath, who'd dived in after James, whilst his colleague had raced in pursuit of Ross. He swam alongside them, not attempting to interfere, as James expertly steered Kits towards the bank.

The officer scrambled out first, quickly reaching down again to pull Kits to the safety of the towpath. James threw himself down on the ground beside her, both of them coughing and trembling.

They lay, still quietly dazed, as people began to gather round, all seemingly talking at once. Their parents. Police officers. Ambulance staff.

James wanted to answer their questions but couldn't. He managed to nod when asked if he could walk, only to find it wasn't true. His legs felt thin, floppy, useless, like dangling strands of spaghetti and he needed two people to support him.

As he was lifted into the ambulance, he knew for a moment how Kits must feel, to be almost totally dependent on others. He wanted to say something reassuring as she was strapped onto the ambulance bed, next to his seat, but she was barely conscious and wouldn't have heard him.

He wondered how much she had taken in, back there, on the towpath. Did she know that Lisa was safe and already on her way to hospital in another ambulance? Had she heard that Ross had finally been arrested? That poor Lew had fallen off his bike, yet again?

He wondered where Lewis was now. Whether he was badly hurt. His questions were answered as his father clambered into the ambulance and the door slammed shut.

'Mum's with Lewis. He's a bit shaken. Suspected fracture. They've taken him to hospital in the car.'

James nodded and tried to smile.

'I'm wondering,' said his dad, smiling back at him, 'whether my children are heroes or just idiots.'

'I don't feel too heroic,' mumbled James, finally forcing his mouth into some sort of action. 'So I guess idiots might be nearer the mark.'

*   *   *

Kits looked up as something lumbered through the doorway of her little hospital room. The same room she'd had before. The one with the flowered curtains and washbasin in the corner.

'It's getting a bit crowded,' she said as Paul steered his walking frame nearer to the bed.

'Sorry,' he said, surveying the scene.

Lisa, in her dressing gown, sitting on the edge of the bed. James sprawled in the chair in the far corner. Lewis, in his pyjamas, cross-legged on the floor.

'I can come back some other time . . .'

'No. It's OK,' said Kits. 'It was good of you to come and see all the invalids. This is my friend, Lisa, and the brothers I told you about.'

'Yeah,' said James, getting up and allowing Paul to use his chair. 'We made a bit of a block booking. Only Kits gets special treatment. The rest of us are supposed to be on the main ward.'

'I read about it all in the paper,' said Paul. 'Amazing. Absolutely amazing. I'm surprised you all look so well.'

'Call this well?' said Lewis, trying to wave his plastered arm in Paul's direction.

'N–no . . .' stammered Paul. 'But I mean after everything you've been through . . .'

'Oh, don't mind him,' said Kits. 'We've had three days to recover but Lew likes to make a big deal of it and get all the nurses fussing over him. All because he was stupid enough to fall off his bike.'

'It wasn't just that, though,' said Paul, as Lewis started to protest. 'I mean going after the bloke like that. Managing to find Lisa. Lewis phoning the police. It was incredible! You know the head-mistress did an assembly about it, Kits. About how you didn't let your disability stand in the way of helping Lisa.'

'I bet she did! Cripples fight back! It would be just up her street, that would,' said Kits, but not bitterly as she might once have done. 'Anyway I was only doing what she suggested . . . She said I should try swimming, so I did but I don't think I'll try it again.'

'Oh,' said Paul, clearly disappointed.

'Not in the canal, I mean,' Kits explained. 'But I might give it a go in the pool. Especially now I've seen you with that,' she said, pointing to his frame. 'Looks a lot more fun than a wheelchair. And besides, mine's about as mangled as Lewis's bike.'

James smiled and winked at Lisa, as Kits chattered on. Grandad David always used to say that good could come from disasters. James had never believed it until now. But the accident had thrown him and Lisa together. The kidnapping had made him realize just how much she meant to him. How much he'd grown to care about her. And then, despite all the worry, despite being dragged from a freezing canal, Kits was so much better. Not

171

physically. Not yet. But her attitude had changed.

Maybe it was knowing that Ross was safely locked away. That he would be in a secure psychiatric prison for a long, long time. Maybe it was the news that Lisa's mum had been persuaded to let Lisa transfer to Stangate which had cheered Kits up. Or maybe it was that Kits was free of the dreams, the visions, the strange powers which had troubled her. She had told him that, this morning when he'd come in to see her and heard her talking in her sleep.

'Goodbye, Grandad,' she'd said.

She had smiled placidly when James had questioned her.

'Don't look so worried. I was having a dream, James. An ordinary dream. It's all gone now. All the funny stuff. I reckon the shock of being hurled into the canal brought me back to my five normal senses. I can't float and I can't make things move. OK? If I want to pick up my own pencils I'll have to try a bit harder with the physio exercises, won't I?'

It would take time. James knew that. There were no instant cures. Not for Kits. Not for little Toby. Not for Lisa. They'd all have to be patient. He looked at Lisa twisting strands of hair around her fingers. Looked down at his own hands. Nails bitten to pieces. Looked up again. Saw Lisa look back and smile. Nothing had really been said between them. But they both knew.

'OK,' a voice said from the doorway. 'This is a hospital not a youth club. Back to your own beds. It's gone nine o'clock. Katherine needs to rest.'

The nurse smiled, ignoring their protests as she ushered them out. Paul was the last to leave.

'Can I come and see you again?'

'You'll have to make it soon. James and Lew are allowed home tomorrow and I don't intend lying around here for much longer.'

'Great,' he said. 'You never know . . . you still might make it into the football team.'

Kits smiled as she heard his frame thumping along the corridor. Football, netball, tennis . . . maybe they'd only ever be memories, but there were other things to do, other ways to grow.

She looked at the chair where Paul had been sitting. There was a white envelope lying there. A card? Had he left her a card? She glanced at her watch. Five minutes before the nurses came with the last tablets of the day. There was time.

She stared hard at the envelope, pulling it towards her with her eyes, her mind.

OK, so she had lied to James. But it was for the best. She didn't want them all worrying, fussing over her, treating her like a freak.

She wasn't a freak. Everyone was different. Everyone had disabilities and talents of some sort. You just had to make the best of what you'd got.

She allowed the envelope to drop onto the bed.

Picked it up. Tore it open. Looked at the dozens of signatures from staff and kids at Stangate. Looked particularly at the one from Paul. Written in bright green ink so she wouldn't miss it. He was OK was Paul. More than OK. Maybe, when she was better . . . She studied his signature. Wondered if her little gifts would allow her to see her own future. Stopped herself, as images began to form.

Sometimes it was better not to know.

THE END

If you enjoyed this book, you might well enjoy another title by Sandra Glover . . .

The
NOWHERE
BOY

SANDRA GLOVER

Turn over for a chance to read the first
gripping chapter . . .

CHAPTER ONE

They came at night. Another emergency. Mandy lay on her bed, the sound of their voices making the learning of French verbs impossible. She closed her book and listened. She knew who they were. Sue Jenson and Mike Patty. Social workers. And, though she couldn't hear their words, the message was clear enough. They had brought a child. Another girl or boy for her parents to foster. One of the temporary sisters and brothers who had been her companions for as long as she could remember.

Mandy sat up, resting her head against the pillows and considered the possibilities. What would it be, this time? A baby? She liked babies. She could make silly cooing noises at them when she felt like it but otherwise they didn't interfere with her life. Except when they kept her awake with their crying. Automatically her hand stretched out and opened the bedside drawer to check her supply of earplugs. The crying wasn't too bad. At least you could block it out and it usually meant the baby was OK.

It was the quiet ones you had to worry about.

Like Billy. Billy had never cried. Not once in all the three months he had been with them. The bruises, which had covered his little body when he arrived, had healed but there was other, more serious damage. Billy had eventually moved on to permanent, adoptive parents who would care for his special needs but his vacant blue eyes haunted her still and brought tears to her own.

Tears. It nearly always ended in tears for one reason or another. The young kids were the worst. The ones who messed up your clothes and broke all your things. Last year it had been Kylie. An angelic-looking four-year-old who had used the contents of Mandy's make-up bag to paint herself, her dolls and the bedroom wall. Mum had laughed! And, in the end, Mandy had laughed too. She was torn between sadness and relief when Kylie's dad came out of hospital and was able to take her home.

Kylie had been a short-stay child. Like fifteen-year-old Ben who had locked himself in the bathroom with a canister of glue and nearly died. After that, Mum had said she wasn't having another teenager. She did, of course. Sarah, who was OK and Lucy who had 'borrowed' their car. Not that Lucy, at thirteen, knew how to drive. She had got as far as the end of the road before crashing through Mrs Henderson's privet hedge. Though hardly funny at the time, the memory made Mandy smile. Poor Mrs

Henderson. She still wasn't speaking to them. She had been very fond of her privets.

Sometimes, they only had one child. At other times, three or four. Some stayed for months and, in a few cases, years. Rose was with them two years, ten months and four days. She had arrived just after her third birthday, thin, grubby and barely able to talk. On the first night, Rose had wandered into Mandy's bedroom and crawled into bed with her. After that, they had squeezed a spare bed into the corner and there Rose had stayed. Mandy's devoted shadow.

It was Mandy who had taken her to speech therapy every Thursday evening after school. Mandy who had taught her to swim and ride a bike. Mandy who took her to the park and sat through Disney cartoons at the cinema with her. Mandy hadn't even minded being woken each morning by Rose's excited chatter. Each day, her words became more distinct. She was a quick learner was Rose and once she had discovered talking, she didn't stop.

Mandy looked over to the corner. The bed was empty now, save for a discarded pile of clothes. Three months ago, the courts had finally made a decision on Rose's future. She was to live with her grandmother. Not far away. Only the other side of the city somewhere. But it might as well have been Mars. Grandma would allow no contact. She wanted Rose to have a fresh start. To forget.

'Forget,' Mandy muttered out loud. 'Forget! Almost three years and we're supposed to pretend it never happened.'

She took out the photograph of Rose which she kept in her bedside cabinet. Slightly freckled cheeks. Blond hair tied up in the French plait Mandy used to do for her. Pale green eyes which never quite lost their sadness, even when Rose smiled.

Mandy slammed the photograph down. It was so unfair. So impossible. She couldn't keep going through . . . Mandy stopped mid-thought, the voices of the social workers still mingling with those of her parents. Something was wrong. They shouldn't be here. Not any more.

After Rose, she had talked to her parents and asked them to stop fostering. Amazingly, they had agreed, almost without argument. Not so much because she was upset but because she was fourteen now and starting her GCSE exam courses. She would, her dad pointed out, need a bit of peace. Her mum, too, had agreed it was a good time for a break. Within days of making the decision, she had got herself a part-time job in the supermarket and later started an Open University degree.

So what were the social workers doing here at ten o'clock on a Friday night? Mandy glanced at her French verbs and at the unfinished history essay. There was no way she was going to concentrate until she found out what was going on.

She swung her legs over the side of her bed and eased her feet into the soft, furry slippers which made no noise as she walked. She crept out of the room and hovered at the top of the stairs. The voices were clearer now.

'So how's life at the supermarket?' Sue was asking. 'How many days did you say you worked?'

An ordinary enough question but Mandy wasn't fooled. This was no social call. Mike and Sue were far too busy to call on people for a chat. This was business all right. And probably not ordinary business either. If they were hoping to get her mother out of her short retirement, then you could bet it was one of their 'special cases'. One that other foster parents didn't want, or weren't capable of taking on. A battered baby, a withdrawn waif, a neurotic drug abuser. They had had them all in their time. Mum could never resist them. And, in spite of their agreement, Mandy couldn't trust her to resist now.

She walked slowly downstairs, as her mother answered Sue's question with ominous undertones.

'Well, I only work mornings, so I suppose . . . but then, I've got OU essays to do and I have to attend tutorials once a . . . and there's not only me to consider. I mean, it was Mandy who . . .'

Oh, don't mind me, Mandy thought bitterly, staring at herself in the hall mirror, pushing strands of light brown hair behind her ears. I'll cope like I always do. Put up with its temper tantrums while it's here, cry for weeks when it goes. She stopped fiddling with her hair, as a thought struck her. What if it wasn't a new child? Sometimes, the old ones came back. What if . . . Rose . . . What if it was Rose?

She advanced silently towards the lounge, all ill humour banished in this sudden hope. She was in luck. The lounge door was open slightly. Just enough to peep in to assess the scene before committing herself to action.

As she approached, a black-and-white border collie shuffled out to greet her. Meg might be old, but her senses were still sharper than any human. Mandy put her hand down to stop the dog making too much fuss and positioned herself in the doorway.

A single glance was enough to banish all optimism. It wasn't Rose who stood, immobile in the centre of the room, her back to the door. It was an older girl, about her own age, she guessed. Dressed in black. None too clean. Dark hair tied back in a pony tail.

'I know it's awkward,' said Mike, stroking his ginger beard and leaning forward in the armchair to stare at her parents who were sitting together on the settee. 'And I take on board what you're saying, Mrs Jones.'

'Only we don't have many options,' said Sue,

also leaning forward from her chair in a two-pronged attack. 'We wouldn't ask if . . .'

'No, I'm sorry,' said Mandy's mother, rather less firmly than Mandy would have liked. 'We can't take him.'

Him! Mandy looked again. Not a girl. Oh, well, an easy mistake to make, with the pony tail and shapeless one-piece outfit it was wearing. He, not it, she corrected herself.

'Alan?' Sue said, appealing to Mandy's father.

'It's up to Cath,' came his predictable reply. 'And Mandy. We'd have to ask Mandy.'

It was time to make an entrance.

'No,' said Mandy, stepping into the room, with the dog at her heels.

The boy didn't move. Mandy had expected him to turn round. To show some interest in this new arrival. But he didn't. He continued to face Sue, forcing Mandy to cross the room and position herself by Sue's chair to get a better view. She was vaguely aware that Sue was speaking to her but Mandy's attention was already firmly fixed on the boy.

It was difficult to know which was the more striking, his face or his bizarre clothes. He was what Mandy's friends might have called an individual dresser. The tight, black one-piece, with no obvious signs of buttons or zips, might have looked fashionable in the sixties. It was held, in the middle, by a black belt with a large silver –

what? Mandy supposed it was some sort of buckle but it was solid, like a box. Round his right wrist was a thick bangle of similar solid design and on his left, one of those heavy multi-purpose digital watches which doubled as calculators. Every centimetre of his body was covered, from his feet, encased in thick, black boots, to the tips of his fingers covered by silky, black gloves. The weirdest thing, though, was that everything seemed to have a fine coating of thin, grey dust, as if the boy and his clothes had recently been taken down from a shelf where they had lain, neglected, for years.

'So we thought, if he could spend time with someone about his own age he might . . .'

'What?' said Mandy.

'His own age,' Sue repeated. 'We think he's about fourteen or fifteen.'

'Oh, yes,' Mandy muttered, before returning her attention to the boy's face.

There was something about it which disturbed her. Something she hadn't quite been able to place. It was an attractive sort of face, if you ignored the grime. High cheekbones, darkish complexion, nice straight nose, brown eyes. Brown eyes, Mandy's brain repeated. Not dark brown like Sue's nor hazel like her own. In fact, if she had to compare them to anybody's in the room, it would have to be Meg's. The boy's eyes were like the dog's. Brown, almost orange and hardly any white showing. There was far too much colour. Mandy wondered whether his vision was impaired by this strange defect. She thought not. At least not close up. He seemed to be seeing her clearly enough. His face was impassive but behind the eyes there was action. He was seeing and assessing, just as she was.

'I'm Mandy,' she said abruptly, deciding to break the silence between them which threatened to become permanent.

His head moved to one side, rather like Meg's would have done, but he didn't reply.

'He doesn't understand English,' Sue said.

'Oh,' said Mandy.

She looked again at the dark skin. He could be anything. Italian. East European. Asian possibly. 'What does he understand?'

'Er — nothing,' said Mike. 'As far as we can make out. We've tried all the obvious ones.'

'Well, where does he come from?' Mandy asked. 'His family must speak something.'

'There isn't a family,' Sue explained. 'At least none we know about. Police picked him up, trying to break into a car in the city centre, apparently. Couldn't get a word out of him. Nothing worth charging him with, so they handed him over to us.'

'Oh,' said Mandy, again.

'He was pretty filthy when they found him.'

'Still is!' said Mandy.

'We've cleaned him up a bit,' said Mike apologetically. 'Can't get him to wash, though, or take his clothes off. Not even the gloves. We got a doctor in to examine him but the boy went wild. We'd have to sedate him to get near him and we don't really want to do that unless absolutely necessary.'

'Of course not!' said Mandy's mother. 'I'm sure he'll be fine if . . .'

She paused. Mandy raised her eyebrows in warning. This was a special case, all right. And if she didn't make her feelings very clear she'd be lumbered with a new foster brother who didn't talk and smelt like the contents of their dustbin.

'No,' she said. 'No, Mum. You promised!'

BREAKING THE RULES
Sandra Glover

'*You might as well send a shark to work in a swimming pool . . .*'

When rebellious Suzie Lawrence is placed for two weeks of work experience at an old people's home, everyone expects the worst – she is more used to breaking the rules than looking after a bunch of ancient wrinklies.

But Suzie rises to the challenge in her own uniquie way, and as she fights a few battles – particularly with the fearsome Matron – everybody's lives are shaken up. Sometimes, rules are made to be broken.

Both funny and moving, this is a thought-provoking novel by the author of *The Nowhere Boy:*

'**It will captivate children and teenagers alike with its skilful and imaginative plot, crisp dialogue and realistic characters.**'
Yorkshire Evening Press

'**Glover handles serious social issues with a humorous touch, writes lively dialogue and has a sympathetic view of youthful idealism.**'
Books for Keeps

0 552 546763

CORGI BOOKS

SOLO ACT
Helen Dunwoodie

*Iris has the looks, the voice, the confidence . . . so why
is everything going wrong for her?*

First Jimmy Garcia, the new (and *very* fanciable)
director of her drama group, has the nerve to
criticize her acting. In front of everyone! Then,
when he announces his plan to take their show
to the world-famous Edinburgh Fringe Festival,
Iris's mother starts being really difficult
about her going.

Iris *knows* she's good enough to make it – and
knows that stardom doesn't come easy. But why
does it have to be *so* hard?

**'Dunwoodie sweeps the reader along in a
most agreeable and enjoyable way'**
Books for Keeps

**'An all-round excellent read for the stage-
struck and those looking for a deeper
account of human relationships'**
Carousel

ISBN 0 552 54524 4

CORGI BOOKS

A.N.T.I.D.O.T.E.
Malorie Blackman

'*The words exploded from me in a burst of white-hot anger. 'It's a lie.'*

It's a normal Friday evening for Elliot – until the police knock on the door and tell him his mum's in serious trouble! A security video clearly shows her breaking into a giant pharmaceutical company on behalf of A.N.T.I.D.O.T.E., the environmental action group.

Elliot can hardly believe it. His mum's a secretary, isn't she? Not a SPY! And even worse – now she's gone on the run . . .

'Malorie Blackman has successfully rebooted the ripping yarn'
The Times

'A gripping techno-thriller'
Independent on Sunday

ISBN 0 552 52839 0

CORGI BOOKS

PIG-HEART BOY
Malorie Blackman

Cameron is thirteen and desperately in need of a
heart transplant when a pioneering doctor
approaches his family with a startling proposal.
He can give Cameron a new heart – but not from a
human donor. From a *pig*.

It's never been done before. It's experimental, risky
and *very* controversial. But Cameron is fed up with
just sitting on the side of life, always watching and
never *doing*. He *has* to try – to become the
world's first pig-heart boy . . .

**'A powerful story about friendship, loyalty
and family around this topical and
controversial issue'**
GUARDIAN

'A tale of courage stretched to the limit'
T.E.S.

MADE INTO A BAFTA
AWARD-WINNING TV SERIAL

0 552 528412
